SAND, SEA AND A SKELETON

DUNE HOUSE COZY MYSTERY SERIES

CINDY BELL

CONTENTS

ISBN: 9781692378516

CHAPTER 1

Suzie Allen fluffed the pillow between her hands, then inspected it closely, before she placed it on the top of the bed. She stared at it for a moment, then picked it up again, and fluffed it again.

"Suzie?" Mary Brent laughed as she stepped into the room. "What exactly are you doing to that pillow?"

"I don't know." Suzie sighed, as she set the pillow back down. Then she edged it a little closer to the other pillow. "It just seems like it's not right."

"It doesn't have to be perfect. Our guests will sleep on it happily no matter what." Mary brushed her gray-streaked auburn hair back over her shoulders and took a deep breath. "So, do you want to tell me what's really going on?"

"Nothing is going on. You're right, I'm just a little too focused on these pillows." Suzie laughed and shook her head as she started towards the door. "I just woke up in a funny mood today."

"Do you want to take a walk with me and Pilot? Maybe we can talk a bit." Mary tried to meet her friend's eyes. She noticed that Suzie's brassy gold hair hadn't been brushed, yet. It was still early, just past eight, but it wasn't like Suzie not to brush her hair and put on makeup before she came out of her room in the morning.

"I'm a little too tired for a walk, I think." Suzie ran her hands back through her hair, then stretched her arms above her head. "I think I'll just lay down for a bit before the guests get here. Enjoy your walk, Mary." She smiled and gave her friend a light pat on the shoulder as she walked past.

Mary watched as she stepped out into the hallway. She opened her mouth to say something more but decided against it. Suzie could be a very private person when she wanted to be, and Mary didn't want to press her. She descended the stairs into the kitchen, then summoned Pilot with a slap against her thigh.

SAND, SEA AND A SKELETON

"Pilot, let's go boy."

The yellow Labrador bounded into the kitchen. His tongue hung out of his mouth as he seemed to grin at her. "Yes, it's time for our walk, buddy. It looks beautiful out there." Mary slid her feet into her slip-on shoes then stepped out through the side door off the dining room. It led to the wraparound porch that surrounded Dune House, a bed and breakfast that she and Suzie had renovated and reopened together after Suzie inherited the large house and property from her uncle.

Pilot raced down the steps from the porch to the sand that stretched to the edge of the crystal blue water. Mary took a deep breath of the salty air and marveled at the fact that she lived in a place she considered paradise. No, Garber wasn't some tropical island, but it might as well have been, as much as Mary loved it. It was a small, seaside town, with most of its locals being long-time residents. Suzie and Mary were transplants, best friends that had lived very different lives, and still ended up under the same roof together.

Mary gripped the railing of the steps as Pilot ran ahead of her. She eased herself down to the sand and did her best to ignore the pain in her knees. Walking had become part of her daily routine as she tried to improve the muscles that supported her knees. Though it always started out painful, the slosh of the waves against the sand, and Pilot's joyful barks took her mind off it. Today however, her thoughts returned to Suzie. What was weighing on her mind that she didn't feel she could share with Mary? They had shared so much of their lives, from Suzie's career as an investigative journalist shifting into a desire to be an interior decorator, to Mary's huge decision to walk away from an unhappy marriage. They had always been able to confide in each other.

Pilot bolted close to the edge of the water, then raced back as a wave rushed towards him. He yelped, then barked at the water.

"That's right, Pilot, you show it who's boss." Mary laughed, and continued to walk along the water.

"Mary." A voice in the distance surprised her. Usually, her morning walks were fairly quiet, especially since the water was starting to get too cold for a swim. Her eyes locked to a familiar face as he jogged towards her.

"Wes." Mary smiled as she walked towards him. She laughed as she noticed he was even wearing his cowboy boots in the sand. "What are you doing out here? Don't you have to work today?"

"Not today. I switched shifts with another detective. He needed the day off for his kid's ball game." Wes offered her his arm. "I thought I'd join you for your walk."

"Why didn't you come to the house?" Mary wrapped her arm around his and smiled to herself. It was still quite an adjustment for her to have a love interest in her life. After her divorce was final, she doubted that she would ever want to be in a relationship again. But Wes, with his patient insistence, had worked his way into her heart.

"Oh, I just thought I'd wait out here and surprise you." Wes cleared his throat, then gestured to a small table and foldable chairs that he'd set up. "For breakfast."

"Breakfast?" Mary's eyes widened. She didn't have the heart to tell him that she'd had breakfast two hours before when she'd woken up. She tended to be an early riser. Still, the romantic gesture stunned her. "Wes, you didn't have to do all this."

"I wanted to." Wes slid his arm from hers and took her hand instead. "Will you join me?"

Mary bit into her bottom lip. There were still a few more things to get ready for the guests, and she liked to be prepared far ahead of time, but she knew that Wes would be disappointed if she turned him down, and she did want to have breakfast with him.

"Sure Wes. I'd love to. Thank you so much for all of this."

"Anytime." Wes winked at her, then reached into his pocket with his free hand. "Don't worry, Pilot, I didn't forget you." He gave Pilot a treat and tossed a ball for him to chase after.

As Mary settled at the table, she noticed that Wes had attempted to make French toast. It was more egg than bread, a bit soggy, and cold, but it made her smile wider than she thought she could.

"You cooked?"

"Not well." Wes grinned as he sat down across from her. "I know you're the chef of Dune House, so I can't possibly compare, but I thought it would be nice if someone cooked for you for a change."

"It is nice." Mary gazed into his eyes. "All of this is very nice. Thank you, Wes."

"Don't thank me." Wes reached across the table and took her hand. "This is what you deserve, Mary. I intend to show you that, every chance I get."

Mary's heart skipped a beat in response to his words. What she deserved? She swept her gaze over the French toast and orange juice that he poured.

Then she looked back into his warm eyes. It was one thing to enjoy his company, it was quite another to start to believe that she could be treated this way for the rest of her life. Careful Mary, she closed her eyes briefly. Don't believe it too much, but enjoy it while it lasts.

Mary picked up her fork and dug into the French toast. She knew that it wouldn't matter how it tasted, she would savor every bite.

Suzie checked on a few of the other guest rooms, then headed downstairs into the kitchen. She guessed that Mary would have found Wes by now. She smiled at the thought of the two of them sharing breakfast on the beach. Mary never would have expected it, and that was exactly why she needed it. Suzie took stock of the contents of the refrigerator in an attempt to decide whether she needed to run to the store before the guests arrived. Satisfied with the milk and water supply, she turned her attention to the pantry. It wasn't easy to keep a secret from Mary. She'd taken extra time on the guest rooms to make sure that Mary didn't go out for her walk too early. She didn't join Mary for her walk so that she wouldn't be a third wheel. Suzie just hoped that Mary enjoyed herself.

As Suzie walked through the dining room, she checked to be sure that the chairs were positioned correctly. First impressions were important to a new group of guests, and this particular one she hoped to impress quite a bit. The five incoming guests were members of a national walking group, and they were trying out Garber as a destination to add to their map of locations around the country. If they added it, then Dune House would be guaranteed a group of guests a few times a year. Though business had been good, it never hurt to generate more.

Suzie continued on into the living room and surveyed the couches and overstuffed chairs. Plenty of natural light filtered through the windows, the largest of which faced the other side of the property, which blended into woods in the distance. For a moment she imagined her late uncle in this living room. He had let the house get rundown and had become a bit of a recluse. He rarely left the house. She'd redecorated the space from the ground up, but that window still had the same view. Had he ever imagined his beloved home becoming a bed and breakfast, once again? As unfriendly as he was, she doubted it.

Suzie turned back towards the front hallway just as someone knocked on the door. She glanced at the time on a large wall clock in the foyer. It was far too early to be the guests. When she opened the door, she smiled at the sight of her cousin. Detective Jason Allen.

"Good morning, Jason. What are you up to?"

"Just making my rounds." Jason shrugged. "I thought I'd stop by and say hello."

"You know you don't have to knock." Suzie waved him inside.

"I didn't want to startle you, it's still early." Jason stepped inside and pulled off his hat. His badge caught the sunlight that poured in through the windows and sparkled.

"Early?" Suzie laughed. "Not around here, it isn't."

"Ah yes, early to rise." Jason winked at her. "I hear you're expecting guests today."

"Yes, a walking group. I meant to ask you if you had any recommendations for areas that they could explore. I know all of the marked places, but you grew up around here, I thought perhaps you discovered some things that aren't on the map." Suzie walked towards the kitchen. "Coffee?"

"Sure, thanks." Jason followed after her. "Yes, I did quite a bit of exploring when I was younger."

"Younger." Suzie scoffed. In his early thirties, he was twenty years her junior, and she had a hard time seeing him as anything other than a teenager. "You're still young, Jason."

"All right, all right. Whatever you say." Jason grinned as he took the cup of coffee from her. "But there are a few places they might want to see. I haven't been out on the trails in a long time, though, so I can't guarantee what shape they're in."

"These people seem like the adventurous type. I'd just like something to wow them with." Suzie grabbed a pad of paper from the kitchen counter and a pen from the can on the breakfast bar. "The man that booked the rooms mentioned that he had heard about a waterfall in the area, but I can't find it on any maps. Do you know anything about a waterfall? I'd really like them to want to come back."

"Got it. There are a few trails that run close to the water." Jason rattled off some addresses of the trailheads. "They are basically just flat trails that lead to some beautiful sights. But there is one other trail that I know of that goes deep into the woods by a waterfall. That might be the one they are talking about. When I was a kid my dad always warned me to stay out of that area, but of course I didn't listen."

"Of course." Suzie rolled her eyes and smiled.

"It's a good thing I didn't, because there is a stunning waterfall back there. It's small, but there's something well—" Jason cleared his throat. "I think, almost magical about it."

"Magical huh?" Suzie raised an eyebrow.

"I took Summer out there not long after we started dating." Jason's cheeks flushed. "Maybe that's why it seems that way."

"Aw." Suzie did her best not to gush over how sweet she found him. "That sounds like the perfect place to take them. How do I get to it?"

"You have to start out behind the post office. The trail doesn't actually start until you go into the woods several feet, and it might be a little overgrown, but there is a huge, gnarled tree right next to it. You can't miss it." Jason glanced at his watch. "Oops, I'm running behind now. Can I take this to go?"

"Of course." Suzie looked up from her pad of paper. "Do you have any idea why your dad warned you not to go out there?"

"There's a mine out there. It shut down when I was a kid. He was probably just worried about me

CINDY BELL

getting into something I shouldn't. I don't know why he would worry about that." Jason grinned, then waved to her as he headed for the door.

"Thanks Jason." Suzie made another note on the notepad and smiled to herself. Yes, a secret waterfall would be exactly the right bait to draw a group of adventurous hikers back time and time again. In fact, she was excited to see it for herself, and she knew that Mary would enjoy it, too.

Suzie set down the pad of paper and stepped back into the dining room. The wall that faced the porch was made up of mostly windows and glass doors. It gave a nice view of the water. She couldn't see too far down the beach, but her gaze settled on the sea. She wondered how Paul's fishing run was going. He was due to dock that night, and she couldn't wait to see him. She wondered if he knew anything about the waterfall. If not, perhaps she could surprise him with a walk out there.

Suzie's smile widened as she saw Pilot run across the sand towards the porch. Mary and Wes weren't too far behind him. They strolled arm in arm. Suzie pulled out her phone and snapped a quick picture of the happy couple. Certainly, neither Mary nor Suzie expected to find romance when they moved to Garber, but it had turned out that

12

way none the less. She was about to step onto the porch to greet them, when she heard a knock at the door.

"Did you forget something, Jason?" Suzie walked over and opened the door. "Oh, hello." She smiled at the five people gathered there, along with their luggage. "I didn't expect you for another hour or two."

"Don't even get me started!" The tallest man of the group huffed. His long, red hair was tied back in a ponytail, and a scruff of beard covered his chin and cheeks. "It has been a rough morning."

CHAPTER 2

"*C*alm down, Sam, we're here aren't we?" The woman who stood beside him was at least a foot shorter, with dark, curly hair. Her wide, brown eyes gazed apologetically at Suzie. "Please excuse him, he doesn't deal well with surprises. Our travel plans got a little jumbled at the last minute."

"A little jumbled doesn't exactly describe it, Tiff." The woman beside her hauled a large duffel bag over her shoulder. She was on the curvier side, with thick, blonde hair and a bright smile. "I think we're all a little frazzled."

"Speak for yourself, Dawn." A broad-shouldered man took the duffel bag from her and slung it over his own arm. His hair was short, slick, and perfectly combed. "I'm ready for a great adventure." He thrust his hand towards Suzie. "Dalton Pride, I'm the leader of this group. Sorry for the early arrival."

"Oh, it's no problem, please come in." Suzie stepped aside as the group of mostly thirty-somethings filed through the door. The last man in the group appeared to be closer to her age. He wore an explorer cap, and had a bottle of sunscreen in one hand.

"Hi there, I'm Charles. You can call me Charlie if you like." He smiled at Suzie as he stepped past.

"Welcome Charlie." Suzie smiled at him. "I'm Suzie."

Mary opened the dining room door and Pilot bolted through it, full of sand and a bit of spray from the water.

"Pilot, sit!" Suzie commanded just before he would have collided with the guests.

"Oh Suzie, I'm sorry. I didn't realize that the guests had arrived." Mary frowned as she grabbed Pilot's collar. "He's a little wound up from the walk."

"It's all right." Suzie smiled. "Everyone, this is Mary, and our resident mascot, Pilot." She looked over at the guests. Although they made it clear on their website that the bed and breakfast was dog friendly, and they mentioned it when the guests booked, and there was even a biography page about

Pilot, she always worried a little that guests would be surprised by his presence.

"Oh, what an adorable little pup!" Tiffany crouched down and offered her hand. "Aren't you just the sweetest?"

"Is there somewhere I can put my bags?" Sam frowned.

"Yes, that would be good." Dalton adjusted the bags on his shoulders.

Dawn had her nose in her phone and appeared oblivious to the rest.

"If you'd like to leave them by the stairs, I can take them up later, or if you'd prefer, I can show you to your rooms, now." Suzie gestured towards the stairs in the kitchen.

"That would be best." Sam nodded. "I could use a few minutes of rest."

"Great. Mary, can you show Dawn and Charlie to their rooms, and I'll take Sam, Tiffany, and Dalton to theirs. Okay?" Suzie smiled at her friend.

"Yes, of course." Mary glanced over her shoulder at Wes who waited on the porch. She gave him a short wave, then smiled at Dawn and Charlie. "Your rooms are just up here." She guided them up the stairs.

Suzie led the other three guests up an additional flight of stairs.

"Each room has its own unique design. I tried to put you in the rooms that I thought you would like, but if you would like to change rooms or need anything, please feel free to let me know." Suzie pointed to the first room by the stairs. "Dalton, this one is yours." She pointed to the next door down the hallway. "Sam, I have you in this room. Then the next door is the linen closet, and Tiffany, your room is across the hall over here." She pointed to the door that led to her room. "I stay upstairs in the room at the end of the hallway, so if you need anything at all please just let me know."

"Thanks so much." Tiffany headed for her room, while Dalton and Sam disappeared into theirs.

Suzie lingered for a moment to see if there would be any immediate discontent. When she was met with silence, she headed back down the stairs to the kitchen.

Mary had her head in the refrigerator.

"Did everything go smoothly?" Suzie stepped farther into the kitchen.

"Yes, Dawn and Charlie seem happy with their rooms." Mary pulled out a platter of snacks she had prepared that morning. "I'm so sorry I wasn't here,

Suzie, I know you said you wanted to lie down, and then I went out onto the beach, and Wes was there and he had planned this amazing breakfast and—"

"Mary." Suzie took the tray from her hands. "I wasn't really planning to nap. I knew all about Wes waiting for you on the beach." Suzie grinned as she carried the tray out to the dining room table. "Please don't worry about not being here, everything is fine."

"Seriously?" Mary grabbed some bottles of water from the refrigerator. "Are you telling me you knew about this the whole time?"

"Well, Wes was a little nervous." Suzie laughed. "Romance doesn't exactly come naturally to him, does it? He thought you might take one look at the table and run the other way. I reassured him that you would enjoy the gesture."

"Suzie." Mary huffed as she placed the bottles of water on the table. "You had me completely fooled. I thought something was weighing on your mind that you didn't feel comfortable telling me."

"I'm sorry, I didn't mean to worry you." Suzie gave her a quick hug. "So, how was breakfast?" She glanced towards the porch. "Is he still out there?"

"No, I told him we would be busy with the guests, so he headed home." Mary blushed as she gazed out at the beach. "He made French toast. It was delicious because he made it specially, but I think he needs some cooking lessons."

"Paul and Wes could learn together." Suzie laughed as she walked back into the kitchen to get a few plates. "I'm happy you had a nice time."

"I did." Mary set some napkins on the table. "But I think next time I'll do the cooking."

"Good idea." Suzie smiled.

Mary looked towards the door as Dawn and Charlie headed for the dining room. "After such a rough start to the day, maybe some snacks will make it better?" She smiled at them.

"Oh yes, thank you." Dawn grabbed a plate. "I'm starving."

"Is that blue cheese?" Charlie pointed at the cheese. "My favorite."

"Yes, it is." Suzie smiled.

As the other three guests joined them in the dining room, Suzie grabbed her pad of paper from the breakfast bar. "I've got a few tips on some places that you might like to explore while you're here."

As Suzie described the trails to the group, they all seemed interested. When she got to the last option, wide eyes stared at her.

"So, there really is a secret waterfall around

here?" Dalton nodded as he smiled. "I'm all over that."

"But these trails are not maintained or marked. After Dalton mentioned the waterfall to me, I asked about it. I was told about this spot by someone who grew up here and knows the town well, but even he hasn't been out there that often." Suzie glanced around at them. "If you'd still like to go, I'd love to join you."

"Me, too." Mary piped up. "Unless, you'd all prefer to go alone."

"The more the merrier." Charlie clapped his hands.

"But you'll have to keep up." Sam crossed his arms. "We're pretty serious about our hikes."

"Don't worry, if you need to hang back a bit, I'm always the caboose." Tiffany laughed and waved her hand at Sam. "Sam and Dalton take the lead."

"We'd love to have you join us." Dalton pulled out his phone. "I'll see if I can find the area where the waterfall is meant to be on the trail maps, that way we won't be going in completely blind. Safety is important."

"A little adventure never hurts, though." Dawn gazed at Dalton. "What's the worst that could happen? A bear? Some poison ivy?"

"No bears." Mary laughed. "But plenty of poison ivy."

"Ugh." Dawn shuddered. "I got it a few hikes ago, and I will never go without knee socks and long sleeves again."

"I did warn you." Dalton glanced up from his phone. "It's important to be prepared for the elements."

"I know that now." Dawn blushed, then added a few more crackers to her plate.

"There are some pamphlets with information about the town on the front desk if you'd like them." Suzie smiled. "I'm sure you'll enjoy your time here, but we made a few recommendations of places you might like to visit."

"Thanks Suzie." Charlie picked up a pamphlet.

"Enjoy your snack." Suzie winked at them, then headed back into the kitchen.

"Are you going to meet Paul, tonight?" Mary followed after her.

"Yes, I planned to. But it will be after dinner. You don't mind, do you?" Suzie glanced at Mary.

"No, of course not. I was hoping you would be. I know how much you miss him when he's gone." Mary grabbed a bottle of water for herself.

"It's fine, I enjoy my time to myself." Suzie busied herself with putting dishes away.

"Uh huh." Mary quirked an eyebrow. "It's okay to admit that you miss him."

"Maybe it's okay to admit it to you, Mary, but I'm not so sure that I'm ready to admit it to myself." Suzie laughed. "It's strange, isn't it?"

"It is." Mary lowered her voice. "Sometimes I still wonder how I ended up with Wes."

"He is a lucky guy." Suzie smiled. However, she wondered that about herself as well. She hadn't come to Garber looking for any kind of relationship. But there was Paul, grumpy and rough around the edges, until she got to know him. Then he became a gentleman that wanted nothing more than to spend time with her. It was a bit of a fight at first, but Suzie had eventually accepted that she wanted him to be part of her life.

All through dinner that night, Suzie thought about meeting him, and when it was time to leave, she even felt a little giddy. She hoped his trip had gone well, mainly because she wanted him to be in a good mood. The dock was only a short distance from Dune House, which got its name from its position perched above the town, with several sand dunes bordering it. She crossed the distance in no time and began to pace the length of the dock as she waited. Soon, she noticed Paul's boat come into view.

"Hi beautiful." Paul opened his arms to Suzie as he got off the boat. He gave her a warm hug and a kiss.

"Paul. I need to speak with you." A man waved to him from the end of the dock.

"Ugh, not now." Paul pulled Suzie closer.

"Paul." Suzie frowned and gave him a light shove. She didn't want any spectators.

"Suzie." Paul cupped her cheek, stared into her eyes a moment longer, then turned his attention to the man that approached him. "What is it, Bob? I just got in, I'm a little exhausted."

"Sorry to interrupt." Bob shot a look in Suzie's direction, then looked back at Paul. "I've been trying to reach you, and I heard that you were getting in tonight. I have a business opportunity for you. I'd like to discuss it as soon as possible. Are you free tonight?"

"No." Paul slid his arm around Suzie's shoulders. "Not tonight."

"Paul, it's fine." Suzie patted his chest. "I don't mind."

"I do." Paul cleared his throat. "We can discuss it over breakfast in the morning, Bob. At the diner. All right?"

"It's really rather time sensitive and—" Bob frowned.

"Not tonight." Paul looked straight at the man.

"Okay, fine. Tomorrow morning. Good evening, Suzie." Bob turned on his heel and walked away.

"Who was that, and how does he know my name?" Suzie turned back towards Paul.

"Oh Bob, he's a local businessman. Generational, his father, and his grandfather, all have businesses in the area. He probably wants in on some kind of fishing charter idea. I'd assume he knows your name because you run the most successful bed and breakfast in Garber."

"You mean the only bed and breakfast in Garber." Suzie smiled.

CHAPTER 3

*A*fter enjoying her evening with Paul, Suzie woke up the next morning eager to start out on the hike. Although she was a little nervous about going into areas of the woods that she didn't know, she was very interested in the waterfall. She hoped that she would be able to add it to the list of suggested destinations for people who visited Dune House. Once she was up and dressed, she heard movement from some of the rooms on the second floor. Yes, these people were early risers, too. She headed down to the kitchen and found that Mary had already prepared a light breakfast.

"I can see you're excited." Suzie grinned as she poured herself a cup of coffee.

"I can't wait to go." Mary handed Suzie a plate of toast.

"Good morning, everyone." Dalton smiled as he descended the last step into the kitchen. "Wow, I didn't expect breakfast this early. Thank you so much." He carried his plate to the dining room table, and soon the others followed suit. As the group discussed the hike, Suzie and Mary packed their own backpacks to take with them.

"So, how is Paul?" Mary flashed her a grin.

"He's happy to be home I think." Suzie blushed as she recalled the way he insisted he only spend time with her. It was nice to be made a priority. She wondered how his breakfast with Bob would go that morning.

Mary handed Suzie a bottle of water. "I'm sure he is. Are you ready for this?"

"I'm a little nervous to be honest. I haven't explored the woods around here very much." Suzie poured some food and water into Pilot's dishes. "Jason did say he hadn't been out there in some time."

"If it's too overgrown, we'll turn back. All set?" Mary swung her backpack onto her shoulders.

"Mary, are you sure that you want to do this?"

Suzie grabbed two granola bars and tucked them into her own backpack.

"Yes, I'm sure." Mary frowned as she studied her friend. "If it gets to be too much, I'll just head back."

"I'm sorry." Suzie met her eyes. "I bet you get tired of me asking you that. I just want to make sure that you're okay."

"I understand." Mary took a deep breath, then let it out slowly. "But honestly, I don't want to miss out on life due to these knees. So, I'll do the best I can until I can't anymore."

"Sounds great to me." Suzie gave her a thumbs up just as the rest of the guests filed into the kitchen.

"Today's the day." Dalton's cheerful voice was punctuated by a sharp cough from Charlie.

"Going to need a few cough drops this morning. Something in this area has my allergies kicking up." Charlie patted his pocket. "I've got plenty if anyone needs any."

"Thanks Charlie." Mary smiled at him. "The post office is only a short walk from here. If anyone needs any bottles of water, there are plenty in the refrigerator."

"Thanks." Dawn opened the fridge. "I could use one."

"Me too, please." Sam called out.

"I'm so excited about today." Tiffany fiddled with her phone. "I just hope I can get my camera to work right. My followers are going to love this."

"Tiff is a CurrentSnap celebrity." Dalton grinned.

"CurrentSnap?" Suzie raised her eyebrows.

"It's a social media site where you can post snapshots of just about anything. Only rule is, it has to be uploaded instantly. No filters for editing are allowed," Dalton said.

"Wow, I've never heard of that." Mary raised an eyebrow. "I guess I will have to check it out."

"It's an interesting concept." Suzie nodded. "These days, it's hard to figure out what is real and what is altered. But how can they know if you upload it right away?"

"When a picture is taken, the time is stamped into its data. So, they can compare that time, to the time it was uploaded. If someone challenges the picture, they'll check it, and if it's found to be any more than a minute between the picture and the upload, then it will be removed from the site. People have actually been banned." Tiffany rolled her eyes. "Some take it very seriously."

"Personally, I don't see why anyone wants to be

on CurrentSnap. I don't post any pictures of myself unless I've been edited in them to look my best." Dawn shrugged. "Why shouldn't I?"

"Dawn, you look beautiful as you are, no need for editing." Dalton smiled at her as he accepted a bottle of water from her.

"And some of us just hike for the sake of hiking." Sam adjusted his pack on his shoulders. "Speaking of hiking, are we going to do any of that today, or are we just going to stand around here talking about uploading?"

"I think what Sam is trying to say is that it's time to download some nature." Charlie waved his hand through the air and laughed.

"No, Charlie, that's not what I was trying to say at all." Sam clapped him on the back as he chuckled.

"Let's go. We're losing the morning." Dalton pulled out his phone. "I think I have the trail mapped out pretty well."

Suzie led the way through the door, then waited to lock it behind them. She put Pilot in the fenced-in area of the yard.

"Sorry buddy, you can't come with us this time. I don't know where this trail is going to lead us, and I don't want you getting mixed up in something you shouldn't." Suzie blew him a kiss before he sauntered off towards his kennel.

"Aw, poor pup." Mary slung her arm around Suzie's shoulders as they followed the others down the driveway. "Maybe next time he can tag along."

"Absolutely. Speaking of tag-a-longs, did you invite Wes?" Suzie let the other hikers get a few feet in front of them.

"No, he's working today. He traded shifts yesterday." Mary smiled as she looked over at Suzie. "But this is kind of nice, going on an adventure with my best friend."

"Yes, it is." Suzie called out to the others. "That's the post office up there, the third building on the left."

"Got it." Dalton waved his phone in the air, then veered off down the path that led beside the post office. He stopped as he reached the thick tree line behind the building. "Wow, you weren't kidding when you said there wasn't a trail."

"Nope." Suzie took a deep breath and looked through the dense trees. "Do you want to brave it?"

Mary watched the other guests. She wasn't sure what to make of their expressions.

"I'm going." Sam shrugged and started to make his way through the trees.

"Right behind you." Charlie called out.

Soon, the entire group had begun to file through the trees.

Mary noticed that Suzie hung back at her side. "You can go faster than me, you know? I'll be fine."

"I want to hike with you, Mary." Suzie flashed her a smile. "Otherwise I wouldn't be here. I just hope that Jason's lead pans out. It wouldn't look so good if we got everyone lost in the woods, would it?"

"Definitely not." Mary grinned. "How is Jason going to explain that one when he has to send out a search party?"

"Let's hope it doesn't come to that." Suzie laughed.

"I found the path." Dalton whistled loudly. "It's over here." He waved one hand in the air.

"All right, one less thing to worry about." Suzie winked at Mary.

Mary did her best to speed up and keep pace with the others. More than curious about the waterfall, she couldn't wait to see it, and that helped ease any pain she experienced. As they walked, she drank in the beauty of the trees that surrounded them. It seemed to her that Garber always had a surprise to discover, and it also didn't have any shortage of secrets. In the small town, most people knew everything about everyone, and it hadn't taken long for that same standard to apply to her and Suzie. It was unnerving at times and comforting at others.

"We're almost there." Dalton called back over his shoulder. "It should be up here on the left, I think."

"You think, or you know?" Sam scoffed.

"I can't believe I forgot my bug spray." Dawn smacked the back of her neck, under her ponytail.

"Here." Dalton pulled his bug spray out of his backpack and offered it to her. "Go on, use as much as you like."

"Thanks Dalton." Dawn smiled at him, then began spraying everywhere.

"Watch it, don't get that chemical stuff anywhere near me." Tiffany edged away from her. "I'm telling you, all you need is the right oils."

"Bah, bugs aren't going to hurt you any." Charlie waved his hand through the air.

"No, nothing in the news about ticks spreading debilitating disease, or anything." Sam rolled his eyes. "Are we going or not?"

"Cool it, Sam. We're almost there." Dalton shot him a stern look.

"Shh. I think I can hear it, can you?" Charlie crept closer to the trees along the edge of the path.

"I can." Suzie smiled at the sound of rushing water.

"Me too." Mary's heartbeat quickened with excitement. "Let's have a look."

"I'm ready." Dawn handed Dalton back the bug spray.

"Here we go." Tiffany held her phone up, ready to take a picture.

As they pushed through the brush to get to the waterfall, Mary ignored the pain in her knees, and enjoyed the moment.

"It sure is small." Sam rubbed his hand back across the top of his head.

"But it's beautiful." Tiffany snapped several pictures.

"I wonder if it's warm." Dawn began to kick off her sneakers.

"I wouldn't do that." Charlie warned. "It's not warm enough out for that water to be warm. The water starts getting cool around here pretty much as soon as fall hits and it stays cold until summer."

"He's right." Mary stepped closer to the small pool of water that collected after crashing over a large pile of rocks. "Charlie, are you from around here?"

"Oh no, not exactly." Charlie grinned, then ran his hand through the water. "Icy, but pretty."

"Suzie, this is magical." Dalton glanced over at her. "Thanks for bringing us out here."

"We should go a little farther." Charlie shrugged as he looked past the rocks. "There's another trail. It looks overgrown, but I'm curious to see where it leads."

"Hopefully, somewhere better than this." Sam trudged forward.

"Mary and I will head back." Suzie waved to the others. "Enjoy your exploring."

"If it's okay with you, Suzie, I'd like to keep going." Mary peered down the trail. "I'm curious to see where it leads."

"Okay, as long as you're okay." Suzie cleared her throat.

"I'm fine, I promise." Mary gave her hand a light squeeze, then followed after the group. Not far along the new trail, Charlie stopped suddenly.

"This way looks interesting." Charlie pulled back some branches to reveal another path.

"It's getting pretty late." Tiffany checked her watch. "We didn't pack lunch."

"We'll be fine." Charlie smiled. "I know Sam's up for it. Aren't you, pal?"

"Always." Sam patted his pack. "I made sure I had enough supplies to last me the day. That's always the best thing to do when you go out for a hike."

"All right, let's take a vote." Dalton held up one hand. "I'd like to go a little farther."

"I would, too." Dawn stepped up beside him.

"Sam and I are both in. What do you say, Tiffany?" Charlie met her eyes.

"I don't know." Tiffany glanced back over her shoulder. "We've really gotten off the main path. Are you sure we can get back?"

"Don't worry." Dalton held up his phone. "I've got the whole thing mapped out."

"Tiffany, if you'd like to go back, Mary and I can go with you." Suzie offered her a smile.

"Yes, it's fine with us." Mary glanced over her shoulder. "But we really aren't too far into the woods. We're closer to the main road than you may realize. It's just over there." She pointed through the trees past the path. "And there's a road that branches off from it that comes through the woods."

"You're right." Suzie nodded. "I almost forgot about that road."

"I guess it will be fine then. Lead the way, Charlie." Tiffany brightened up as she began to walk again.

Suzie glanced over at Mary, and bit her tongue. She knew that her friend didn't want her to question her again about her knees. Instead, she followed after her, as she followed the others down the path.

"What's that?" Sam called out as the others came to a stop. "A door?"

"Looks like it." Charlie drew some vines away from it. "Maybe we should take a look."

"It could be dangerous in there." Tiffany narrowed her eyes.

"Are you going in?" Dawn gazed at Dalton.

"I'm in." Sam pushed past Charlie and stepped through the door.

"Wait!" Suzie called out. "That's probably the old mine that Jason warned me about. I have no idea if it's safe."

"It can't be too bad, we'll be careful." Dalton followed Sam inside, with Charlie right behind him.

Dawn grabbed Tiffany's hand. "Let's go, I don't want to miss out."

"All right, fine." Tiffany scrunched up her nose. "But I don't get a good feeling about this."

"There probably aren't as many bugs." Dawn tugged her forward.

"Let's go, Suzie." Mary started walking.

"Mary, I don't know. Jason said it's been abandoned. His father used to warn him not to go in." Suzie hung back a few steps.

"It's a little adventure. We'll be careful. Besides, we can't let our guests go in without us, can we?" Mary peered through the door.

"You're right. I'd just stand out here and worry." Suzie followed Mary in through the door. She was sure that nothing could go wrong.

CHAPTER 4

"Flashlights everyone." Dalton led the way, though Sam matched his pace. The corridors were sloped so the farther they walked inside the deeper the mine went.

There were many corridors and it wasn't long before Suzie felt completely turned around. She kept that to herself, and hoped that Dalton's phone app would work in the mine.

"Look at this, it's all blocked off with junk." Charlie pulled some old carts out of the way. "But it's definitely another corridor."

"Okay, but this is the last one." Dawn groaned. "My feet are aching."

"Did you wear those inserts I gave you?" Dalton cut a look in her direction.

"No." Dawn winced. "I forgot."

"Let's see what's inside." Sam stepped through the doorway.

Suzie glanced over at Mary.

"We might as well have a look," Mary whispered to her.

Sam shone his flashlight through the narrow corridor they stepped into. He took a sharp breath as the flashlight beam landed on something in the corner.

"What is it?" Tiffany held up her phone and began to snap pictures.

"Is that real?" Sam took a few steps back.

"I'm pretty sure it is." Tiffany gulped. "Oh no!" She clapped her hand over her mouth. "I uploaded it. I have my camera set to upload right away so that I don't miss a chance to post on CurrentSnap."

"Tiffany, your CurrentSnap account isn't the biggest concern right now." Dawn grabbed onto Dalton's arm. "We need to get out of here."

"Is that a skeleton?" Mary's mouth hung open as she stared.

"Wait, maybe it's some kind of prank." Suzie crept closer to the skeletal remains. She crouched down and looked at the necklace that hung around its neck. It looked like a cross of some kind. It was small and golden. It gave no hint as to whether the remains were male or female. However, the tattered shoes that the skeleton wore, were quite large. "I don't think it's a prank." She frowned as she straightened back up. She noticed a duffel bag beside the remains. It was filthy, but she could make out some markings on it. "Dawn is right, we need to get out of here." She looked up at Mary. "Are you okay to walk?"

"I'll do my best." Mary nodded as she forced a smile to her lips.

Suzie could see the strain in her friend's expression.

"Uh, there might be a small problem with that." Dalton held up his phone. "I can't get anything to work. We must be too deep for me to get any kind of signal."

"Are you saying we're lost in here with a skeleton?" Dawn gasped.

"Take a deep breath." Mary placed a hand on Dawn's shoulder. "We can retrace our steps."

"How?" Tiffany frowned. "Dalton was tracking us, none of us paid attention to which way we went."

"We're going to end up like this guy." Dawn

pointed to the skeleton. "Maybe that's what happened to him."

"I doubt it." Sam peered at the chest, where his scruffy shirt had an obviously large stain and hole through it. "Looks like a gunshot wound to me."

"Don't get so close." Suzie stepped towards him. "This is a crime scene. The police will need it as untouched as possible. We need to go."

"How exactly are we going to get out of here if we don't know where here is?" Charlie slid his hands into his pockets. "I don't mean to be a downer here, but apparently we were lost when we found this poor sap, and we're still lost."

"We can start with what we do know." Suzie stepped back out of the corridor and into the next. "We came from that way." She pointed in the direction they had been walking from. "So we go back that way."

"Maybe as we get closer to the surface, my phone will start working again." Dalton frowned as he tapped his finger against it. "It's supposed to get reception just about anywhere."

"I guess they don't include mines in that." Charlie chuckled.

"What kind of mine is this anyway?" Tiffany followed after Suzie and Mary.

"I'm not sure." Suzie shone her flashlight along the corridor. "I can find out for you, though."

"Looks like gold." Charlie pointed his flashlight at his chin and smiled as his face lit up. "Maybe there's some left behind."

"I doubt it." Mary laughed. "But that would be quite a surprise, wouldn't it?"

"Yes. My phone is working again. I'll take the lead." Dalton stepped past them. As they walked through the corridors, Suzie made sure she concentrated on which way they went so that she could get back to the skeleton. Soon they were out of the mine.

As soon as Suzie had service, she pulled out her phone and turned to Mary.

"Mary, can you take the others back to Dune House? I'm going to wait here for Jason, so I can show him what we found."

"Are you sure you'll be okay alone?" Mary asked.

"Yes, of course." Suzie smiled. "Jason will come out here, I'm sure."

"Okay, call me if you need anything." Mary walked off with the others.

Suzie braced herself as she waited for Jason to answer the phone. How would he react to finding out that she'd ignored his warning and gone into the mine? She guessed he'd forget all about it, once she told him what they'd found.

"Suzie, where are you?" Jason's tense voice carried through the phone.

"I'm at the old mine you warned me about. We found something there, Jason, you're going to need to come out here." Suzie took a deep breath and prepared to explain.

"I know you did. I've already gotten four calls about it. I'm on my way to you, now. I'm going to take the road entrance. Is that where you are?"

"You know I did? Did Mary call you? I'm in the woods near an entrance that was blocked by some brush." Suzie glanced around.

"Stay where you are, I will come to you. Yes, I know, and no Mary didn't tell me. It's apparently all over CurrentSnap." Jason sighed. "I wish you would have called me first."

"Are you kidding? I didn't think it would get uploaded that fast. One of the hikers has her phone set to upload to that app as soon as she takes pictures. She took the picture before she realized what she was looking at." Suzie frowned.

"It's all right, apparently the site has already taken it down. Hopefully, not too many people saw it, or that mine will be crawling with people trying to solve the mystery. I'm pulling in now. Let me know when you hear me." Jason ended the call.

Suzie slid her phone into her pocket and began to pace back and forth. Minutes later she heard Jason's voice.

"Suzie? Where are you?"

"Over here, Jason!" Suzie walked towards the sound of his voice.

"Wow, I never even knew there was an entrance over here." Jason jogged up to her. "Are you all right?"

"Yes, I'm fine. I sent Mary and the hikers back to the house, but I can show you where we found the skeleton." Suzie cringed. "Any chance it might still be a hoax of some kind?"

"It's possible, but I'll need to see it to find out. Can you show me how you got in?" Jason peered through the brush.

"Sure, it's right over here." Suzie glanced back at him. "We found the waterfall, Jason."

"I'm glad you did, but I warned you about this place, Suzie." Jason pulled back some branches for her, then continued on.

"I know that, Jason, and I'm sorry. The others wanted to go in and explore, and I didn't want them to be alone." Suzie pointed ahead to the door. "Charlie found that, and then they all wanted to go in. They were going to go whether I was with them or not. I just didn't want to stand out here and worry."

"I understand." Jason glanced at her. "It's a good thing you did go in, I guess. It looks like we have quite a mystery on our hands."

"Do you know who it might be?" Suzie paused at the entrance.

"I'm not sure. No one has been reported missing lately, but of course, this person would have been reported missing long ago. Once Summer has a chance to estimate the age of the bones and how long ago this person might have died, it will give us a better idea of who it might be. I didn't want to call everyone out here until I confirm that it's something that needs to be investigated." Jason pulled back the brush, then followed her into the mine.

Suzie led the way with her flashlight. "We have to pay attention to how we go in, because finding our way out again isn't easy."

"I've never been inside this place." Jason flicked his flashlight in a few different directions. "That was one thing I listened to my father about. Maybe because there were always rumors that it was haunted."

"Why would anyone think that?" Suzie navigated the narrow corridors that led to the pile of carts they had found.

"You know kids, any dark and spooky place gets its own stories. I'm not sure how it got started actually. But by the time I was a teenager it had a pretty solid reputation for being a place you just didn't go." Jason shined his flashlight on the half-blocked door. "Is that it?"

"Yes." Suzie stood back as he stepped in front of her. "It's on the left in the corner. I swear, I thought it had to be a prank at first. But Sam noticed a gunshot hole in the chest."

"Could be." Jason crept close to the skeleton and shined his flashlight on the hole. "It could be other things, too." He sighed. "But it's definitely real. I'd better get the crime scene crew out here, and Summer." Dr. Summer Rose was the local medical examiner and Jason's wife. Jason looked over at Suzie. "I'll walk you back out first. I don't want the information of who it might be getting around." He pulled a roll of yellow tape from his pocket and stuck one end of it to the door, then he unrolled it along the wall as they walked. "This will keep everyone from getting lost."

"Good idea." Suzie frowned. "I guess maybe all the kids were right. This place might really be haunted."

"There was certainly a secret to discover. Please keep the specific details to yourself." Jason stepped back out of the mine with her, then pulled out his phone. "You can go back to Dune House. I'll stop by later to talk to the hikers that were with you."

"Thanks Jason." Suzie gazed at him a moment longer as he put his phone to his ear. She trusted that he would handle it, but her need to know who the skeleton was sent her thoughts racing. There was a time when she would hunt down a story just like this, and her instincts were still trained to dig deeper. As she walked back towards Dune House, she replayed the scene in her mind. The skeleton was seated against the wall, in the corner. Had the person been hiding? The carts were piled up in front of the entrance. Was that intentional? Did someone want to hide what they had done? Since the mine had not been operating for years, was it possible that the remains were placed there after the mine had closed? There were so many possibilities, and she wasn't sure which one to focus on first. But she did know the best place to start. When she arrived at Dune House, she found that Mary had put out a lunch spread for the guests, which they were all happily partaking in.

"Jason is starting an investigation," Suzie murmured to Mary as she met her in the kitchen. "He's going to come by later to talk to our guests, and to give us an update."

"Good." Mary took a deep breath. "I'm sure he will figure all of this out."

"He might." Suzie shifted from one foot to the other.

"Maybe not before you?" Mary smiled. "I can see that investigative itch in you."

"Do you mind if I go to the library and grill our favorite librarian? He seems to know everything that has ever happened in this town." Suzie glanced at the guests. "They all seem pretty content at the moment."

"Absolutely, let me know what you find out." Mary smiled.

"Thanks Mary." Suzie gave her a quick hug, then headed right back out the door. She was sure that Louis would have some kind of insight about the mine, if not about the skeleton that was hidden inside.

CHAPTER 5

*N*ot long after Suzie left for the library, the hiking group decided to head into town. Mary was relieved. She had a lot on her mind, and she could use the rest. She made her way to her room and settled in her recliner. Then she placed two ice packs on her knees and closed her eyes while Pilot slept on her bed. It was the hike from the mine that had done it. She was sure of it. She should have been more careful. As she willed the pain to stop, she recalled the sight of the skeletal remains. How could someone have been hidden away in the mine for so long, and no one know it? Maybe he was a vagrant that had wandered inside and gotten lost, as Charlie had suggested. But maybe he was someone who mattered to someone else.

A knock on Mary's door made her jump. Suzie had gone off to the library, and most of the guests were in town as far as she knew. Who could be outside of her bedroom? Pilot was already at the door. She eased the ice packs off her knees and pushed herself up to her feet. As she made her way to the door, she heard a familiar voice.

"Mary, it's me."

"Wes?" Mary opened the door. "What are you doing here? I thought you were working today?"

"I was. I am." Wes cleared his throat as he patted Pilot's head. "The call about the mine came over the radio. I knew you were headed out that way. I just wanted to make sure that you were okay."

"Oh, I'm fine." Mary managed a small smile. "Nothing to worry about."

"Those ice packs tell me differently." Wes stepped into her room and pointed to her chair. "Sit back down, let's get these back on you."

"No, don't." Mary backed up, flustered by his sudden presence in her room. "I can handle it. Really, it's best if you get back to work, Wes."

"I have some time." Wes guided her down into the chair. "Have you tried elevating your legs?" He grabbed the ottoman and started to lift her legs.

"Ow! No don't, please." Mary's cheeks flushed with a mixture of pain and embarrassment. "I'm fine, just go."

"I'm sorry, Mary." Wes took a step back. "I didn't come here to upset you."

"I know you didn't, Wes. None of this is your fault. I just need some time. Today was a big shock." Mary took a deep breath and placed the ice packs back on her knees.

"I'm sure it was. Jason told me that the remains haven't been identified, yet." Wes ran his hand through his hair. "When the press gets hold of this, they are going to love it. Anything for a mystery."

"It is hard not to be curious about it." Mary sat forward in her chair. "I was there, I saw it, and it was so shocking."

"I'm sure it was." Wes frowned. "How are you handling it?"

"Not shocking in a disturbing way. Not exactly, anyway." Mary adjusted the ice packs. "It was just really surprising, and then instantly, I felt as if I had stumbled upon a secret that was never meant to be revealed. But I also felt so badly for this person, who no one had ever found."

"I understand." Wes nodded.

"I'm not going to be able to let this rest until that

person at least has a name. Suzie went to the library to see what Louis might know about it," Mary explained.

"That was a good idea." Wes strode towards the door. "If I find out anything about this, I will let you know."

"Thanks Wes."

Wes patted Pilot on the head, stepped through the door, then pulled it closed behind him.

Mary returned her thoughts to the skeleton. Maybe she couldn't go hunt down information, but she could do a little searching of her own. She picked up her phone and began to search for any information about the mine, and the stories that centered around it.

Although she didn't come across much, she did find an article that had been uploaded that mentioned a celebration at the mine. They had discovered even more gold than they expected and invited the entire town to a party to mark the discovery. There were many pictures of the entrance of the mine, as well as nearby decorated tables, and people gathered together with champagne glasses in their hands.

Mary zoomed in on the picture and began to look through the faces of the people gathered there.

Did the skeleton belong to one of them? There were a few men in suits, as well as some children, and many other men who wore coveralls. She focused on the men in suits. There were three of them. A young boy stood beside the tallest. The young boy's eyes were focused on a gold nugget he held in his hand, while the men grinned at each other. In the background of the photograph there were a few women gathered. From their expensive dresses, Mary guessed that they were the wives or family members of the owners.

The names of the workers were listed under the photo. She decided that she would look more into that later.

Mary noticed the vast difference between the workers and the owners. While the workers had smudges of dirt on their faces, the men in suits were perfectly clean. It occurred to her that some of these workers might have felt some resentment for the fact that their hard work had provided such a valuable find. Did they benefit from it? Did they get a bonus, or some other kind of reward? It was one avenue to look into.

The person in the mine could have been a worker who got lost, he could have been a vagrant who wandered in for a warm place to sleep. But it also could have been put there by the murderer. This person was Garber's mystery, and Mary was determined to solve it. She pulled the ice packs off her knees and stood up from her chair. There would be time to rest and recover later.

After Mary headed down the stairs into the kitchen with Pilot following her, she bent down to stroke the top of his head, then looked up as the front door opened. Charlie and Sam walked in. They both spoke quietly to each other as they approached. Mary didn't think they noticed her. She stepped towards the back door and tried to listen in on their conversation.

"None of us know what we saw there," Charlie muttered to Sam. "That's all you have to tell the cops."

"They make me nervous. I'd rather just not say anything at all." Sam put his foot on the bottom of the stairs that led to the higher floors.

"Don't do that." Charlie put his hand on Sam's arm and looked up at him. "It will make you look like you're hiding something."

"Whatever." Sam pulled away and continued up the stairs.

Charlie turned away and froze as he looked into the kitchen.

Mary met his eyes as she stepped farther into the kitchen. "Hi Charlie. Hungry?"

"No, I'm not hungry." Charlie studied her for a moment. "Just going for a walk on the beach."

"Would you like some company?" Mary smiled, as her mind raced with the conversation he'd just had with Sam.

"That's all right, I know you need your rest." Charlie nodded to her, then continued into the dining room, and out onto the porch.

Mary watched until he was gone. Had he and Sam just been getting their story straight about the skeleton?

Suzie stepped into the library and spotted Louis behind his desk. As she approached, he looked up and smiled.

"Hi Suzie. How are you today?"

"A little frazzled, actually." Suzie pulled a chair up to his desk and sat down. "Do you have a few minutes to help me out with something."

"Sure, what is it?" Louis turned in his chair to face her. "Another great mystery you need me to solve? Did you pick something up at an antique show for the house?"

"Yes, another great mystery, but no it's not an antique. Well, not exactly." Suzie glanced around to be sure that no one else was within earshot, then spoke in a low voice. "Mary and our guests and I wandered into the old mine today. We found something very disturbing." She glanced around once more, then leaned closer to Louis. "Skeletal remains."

"Of what?" Louis' eyes widened. "I'm sure that many animals could have gotten trapped down there. I've been pushing for years to get the entrances sealed up, but the owners refuse."

"It wasn't an animal, Louis." Suzie took a sharp breath. "We found a human skeleton."

"Eh?" Louis rolled back a bit on his chair. "Are you sure it wasn't some prank? The kids around here are a little crazy these days."

"No, it wasn't a prank. I saw it with my own eyes. Jason has opened an investigation. But I was hoping that you might be able to give me a little information about the mine, and its history." Suzie tipped her head to the side. "You know my curiosity tends to get the better of me."

"That's a polite way of putting it." Louis grinned,

as he studied her. "You're too impatient to wait to see what Jason turns up."

"Yes, that's true, so are you going to help me?" Suzie offered him a warm smile as she met his eyes.

"Of course, I am." Louis turned back to his computer. "Wow, this is going to be quite a scandal around here." His fingers flew over his keyboard, then he nodded. "I knew this already, but just wanted to confirm it. The mine is owned by two men. Terrance Calor, and Donald Laller." He tapped a few more keys, then nodded. "It was closed twenty-four years ago, and the only recent information about the property is that it is up for sale. It was listed a few months ago by Donald Laller."

"Can you tell me anything about him?" Suzie grabbed a piece of paper from the printer beside Louis' computer and pulled a pen from her purse. She jotted down the names of the two men, then looked up at Louis.

"Donald Laller lives in Parish, and it looks like his business partner, Terrance Calor, still lives in France." Louis raised an eyebrow.

"It's interesting that they have the mine up for sale. I guess they had no idea that there was a body in there, otherwise they wouldn't be trying to sell it."

Suzie made a few more notes on the paper, then sat back in her chair.

"Possibly. Often these mines are sold just for the property, and the mines themselves are destroyed. So, maybe they thought it would be the best way to hide their secret." Louis shrugged. "It's hard to say, though. Donald is well into his seventies, it's possible the sale was pushed through because of his son. Robert Laller." He looked over at her. "He also lives in Parish. Maybe he wanted his inheritance early."

"Maybe." Suzie tapped her fingers lightly on the desk. "What about the skeleton itself? Any ideas about who that could be?"

"Well, I was just a kid when the mine was closed. But I remember it caused quite a stir. It was a big boost for the economy around here, and a lot of people lost their jobs. The closure was unexpected." Louis typed a few things into the computer. "Let's see. News from around that time was mostly about the mine closing. Apparently, they had mined most of the gold and there just wasn't enough left to justify keeping the mine open. It was deemed unsafe as well and they couldn't justify fixing it when the gold had dried up. But there isn't anything about someone going missing." He pressed his fingers against his lips and closed his eyes. "Though I do remember something. There was one man that disappeared around that time. His name was Jimmy Tomson." He scrolled through the images on his screen. "It looks like he was in charge of the other workers in the mine."

"So, maybe someone reported him as missing." Suzie frowned as she looked over his shoulder.

"He was never reported as missing as far as I know, but I remember my grandfather mentioning it to my father. He said that it wouldn't be like Jimmy Tomson to just up and leave. But that's all I remember." Louis shook his head as he turned to look at Suzie. "It might not be him, but if I'm not mistaken, the timing is right."

"You remember that after all these years?" Suzie pulled up a chair beside him.

"I'm not just an aficionado of books, I'm an aficionado of memories, too. I was kind of a lonely child. I spent a lot of time with the adults. Plus, I was always looking for something interesting." Louis groaned as he rolled his eyes towards the ceiling. "Growing up in Garber was like watching paint dry."

"Oh, it couldn't have been that bad." Suzie smiled. "Jason grew up here."

"Trust me, ask him about it sometime. It was boring." Louis pointed to a picture on the screen of a man that looked to be in his forties. "That's Jimmy. Obviously, you won't be able to identify him, but I just thought you might want to see him."

"He certainly doesn't look like that anymore." Suzie offered a grim smile as she studied the man in the photograph. He had large shoes, but so did many men. A glint of gold around his neck caught her attention.

"Is that a cross?" Suzie leaned closer to the screen.

"It might be. I can zoom in a little." Louis clicked a few buttons. "Now, it's too blurry, I guess. But it might be. Why?"

"Oh, no reason." Suzie cleared her throat as she recalled Jason's request to keep the specific details to herself for the moment. She understood that he didn't want rumors spreading through Garber about who it might be. "I think you should pass this information on to Jason."

"I'm sure if he really had disappeared, someone would have reported it." Louis picked the picture up out of the printer tray and handed it to her. "Feel free to tell Jason anything you like, then if Jason has any questions he can ask me."

"Sure, okay." Suzie smiled at him. "Thanks for the information." As she walked back out of the library, she gazed at the picture in her hand. Could the skeleton in the mine be Jimmy Tomson? If so, what had happened to him? Who had left him there? She shivered as she wondered how it just happened to be that on that fateful morning they had all decided to go into that mine and managed to find him. Was Jimmy just ready to be found?

CHAPTER 6

*S*uzie stepped through the door of Dune House to find all of the guests and Mary gathered in the living room. Mary met her in the doorway.

"Jason is on his way over. He asked me to gather everyone." She passed a brief glance in the direction of Charlie and Sam who sat together on the couch, with Tiffany perched on one side of them. "Did you find out anything from Louis?"

"He suspects the skeleton might be this man. Jimmy Tomson." Suzie held up the picture of Jimmy. "But he doesn't know for sure. He doesn't think he was ever actually reported missing, so it is just a hunch on his part. He said when he was young, he could remember his grandfather insisting that Jimmy wouldn't have just up and left town, as others believed he did. It's about the right timing. I can't see properly in the photo but that might be the same necklace we saw on the skeleton." She shrugged. "It's not much to go on, but it's a start. How are things here?"

"I think Sam and Charlie are up to something." Mary tugged Suzie out into the hallway. "I overheard them discussing how to handle talking to Jason. Something seems pretty strange about that."

"Hm. I wonder what they could be up to?" Suzie's eyes narrowed. "Maybe there is something they need to hide?"

"I'm not sure." Mary tipped her head towards the front door as it swung open. "But I bet Jason might find out something more."

"Hi Suzie, Mary." Jason nodded to them both as he pulled his hat off his head. "Thanks for getting everyone together. There's a lot of work to do on this case and the faster I can get the statements, the faster I can get back to work."

"Everyone's in the living room." Suzie gestured to the doorway. She started to hand him the picture, but hesitated. It would probably be better to let him talk to the others first. After all, Jimmy Tomson might just be a wild goose chase.

Suzie and Mary observed as Jason spoke to the others as a group. It was clear that he didn't suspect any of them of anything. Suzie couldn't even figure out what there might be to suspect them of doing.

Sam gave one word answers to every question. Charlie recounted every detail, from the narrow corridors to the bullet hole in the chest. Tiffany shuddered every time someone said skeleton, and Dawn picked at the bug bites on her arms while barely responding to the questions. Dalton placed his head in his hands and sighed.

"Listen, this is all my fault. I'm the leader of this group. I never should have led us into that mine. If anyone is going to get into trouble for trespassing it should be me." Dalton looked up at Jason. "Please don't hold it against any of the others."

"Don't worry, Dalton." Jason smiled at him. "No one here is in trouble. I just needed to make sure I had an idea of everything that happened inside of that mine so that we can account for any disturbance of the crime scene. Thanks for speaking with me, everyone." Jason gave his notepad a light pat. "I think I have all the information I need." He stood up and walked towards the door.

Suzie jumped up, with Mary on her heels, and

followed after him. When she caught his arm at the door, he turned to face her.

"What about an update?" Suzie met his eyes.

"Ah yes." Jason glanced at Mary, then back at Suzie. "Why don't you step outside with me?" He opened the door and held it open for them both as they stepped through. Once the door was closed again, he slid his notepad into his pocket. "Listen, this is going to be a sensitive investigation. The press are already involved. So far, all I know for sure is that the skeleton has been there for twenty to thirty years. Summer is going to narrow it down the best she can."

"Wasn't there anything in the duffel bag that would identify him?" Suzie narrowed her eyes. "I thought for sure there would be an ID or something inside."

"Duffel bag?" Jason gazed at her. "What are you talking about?"

"The duffel bag that was right next to the skeleton. It said Lane Street Gym on it, I think. It was filthy but I could make out the outline of the letters." Suzie shook her head. "Didn't you see it there?"

"Suzie. There was no duffel bag." Jason locked his eyes to hers. "You must be confused."

"No, I saw it, too." Mary frowned. "I know I did."

"Well, it wasn't there when you brought me to the skeleton, Suzie." Jason raised his eyebrows. "It couldn't have just disappeared."

"No, it couldn't have." Suzie shook her head. "There must be some mistake. I'm sure Tiffany has a picture of it. Let me check with her." She stuck her head back inside the house and called into the living room. "Tiffany, can I speak to you out here for a second?"

"Sure." Tiffany stepped through the door. She looked nervously at Jason. "Am I in some kind of trouble? I swear, I didn't know we were trespassing."

"No trouble." Jason rested one hand on his gun belt as he studied her. "Suzie said you have a picture of the crime scene."

"Ugh, CurrentSnap took it down after a few minutes because there was more than a minute between the time I took the picture and the picture uploaded. I must not have had any reception down there, either. If they hadn't already removed the photo, I imagine they would have taken it down once they realized what was in the photo." Tiffany pulled her phone from her pocket. "Anyway, I should still have them on my phone." She skimmed through the photographs, then looked up at Jason. Her mouth hung half-open as she looked into his eyes.

"Tiffany, I need to see that picture." Jason shifted a little closer to her.

"I uh. This is impossible." Tiffany looked back down at her phone. "All of the pictures are here of the waterfall, and our walk through the woods. But the pictures from inside the mine are gone."

"Gone?" Jason held his hand out for the phone. "May I take a look?"

"I guess." Tiffany's hand trembled as she handed the phone over.

"Tiffany, are you okay?" Mary wrapped an arm around her shoulders.

"Just a little chilly out here." Tiffany rubbed her hands along her arms.

"It is." Suzie squinted up at the cloudy sky. "It's much cooler than it was earlier."

"I don't see any pictures of the mine on here." Jason frowned as he handed the phone back to her. "Do you remember what was in the picture?"

"A skeleton." Tiffany gulped out the words, then shivered again.

"Anything else?" Mary tightened her arm

around Tiffany's shoulders in an attempt to keep her warm.

"What else was there to remember?" Tiffany shook her head. "I haven't been able to get the sight of that skeleton out of my head."

"What about a bag?" Suzie stepped closer to her.

"Careful Suzie." Jason placed a hand on her shoulder.

"A bag?" Tiffany scrunched up her nose. "No, I don't remember seeing a bag. Can I go back in now? It's cold out here."

"Sure." Jason nodded to her, then watched as she stepped back into the house.

"Jason, you have to believe me." Suzie turned to look at him. "I saw that bag."

"Oh, I believe you." Jason ran his hand along his chin. "I believe that Tiffany had pictures of it, too. I know there were pictures of the skeleton inside the mine on CurrentSnap before they disappeared. So why did she delete them?"

"She didn't say she did." Mary glanced back at the door. "She seemed surprised that they weren't there."

"She also seemed very nervous." Jason looked between both of them. "For now, the information about the bag stays between us. Understand?"

CINDY BELL

"Sure, but why?" Mary frowned. "We were all there. I'm sure other people saw the bag."

"I'm sure they did, too. Because someone must have taken it." Jason lowered his voice. "There may be more to this little adventure into the mine than I anticipated. Just please, keep this information to yourselves."

"Jason, I think this might be the man we're looking for." Suzie held up the picture. "He disappeared around the right time. Jimmy Tomson. It's just a hunch, but I thought I should share it with you."

"Jimmy Tomson?" Jason narrowed his eyes. "I'll look into it." He took the picture from her. "I have to go." He turned and hurried down the front steps.

"That was strange, don't you think?" Mary shifted closer to Suzie. "Do you really think that someone took it?"

"It was there when we found the skeleton and gone by the time the crime scene team got there. I don't remember if it was still there when I took Jason into the mine." Suzie sighed. "I wish I could. But I think Jason must be right. Someone must have taken it."

"But why?" Mary slid her hands into her

74

pockets to warm them. "It had to be as old as the skeleton."

"Maybe to keep the skeleton's identity a secret. Maybe because there was something inside they wanted." Suzie shrugged. "I don't know for sure, but I do know that we're going to have to find out more, before one of our guests ends up being caught up in this investigation."

"You can't leave a mystery alone." Mary winked.

CHAPTER 7

After a late night of researching everything she and Suzie could about the mine and Jimmy Tomson, Mary woke the next morning with a start. She'd slept later than she usually did, and she could hear movement in the kitchen. She wondered if one of the guests was already up. After tossing a robe over her nightgown, she walked with Pilot close behind down the hall to the kitchen and found Suzie in front of the coffee maker.

"Morning Suzie." Mary wiped at her eyes. "I overslept."

"Only you would call waking up at dawn oversleeping." Suzie flashed her a grin. "I had hoped you might sleep a little longer. I know how late you were up last night. I think I'm going to pay a visit to

Donald today and find out what he might have to say about the sale of the mine. Do you mind steering the ship today?"

"Of course not, but I do need to pick up some groceries." Mary glanced up at the clock. "I could probably do that and get back before most of the guests wake up."

"I can go to the store if you want."

"No, it's okay." Mary shook her head. "I'll leave some fruit and muffins out just in case they wake up before I get back."

"Sounds good. I might still be here when you get back. There is no use going to Donald's office so early. I'm just going to get ready and I'll take Pilot for a quick walk." Suzie grabbed an apple from the bowl. "If I'm already out when you get back, I'll give you a call to let you know what I find out."

"Please do." Mary walked over to feed Pilot, then poured herself a cup of coffee. Once she'd had a few sips she headed back to her room to get dressed. When her cell phone buzzed, she glanced at it. A text from Wes indicated he had the morning free.

Mary smiled to herself as she asked if he wanted to join her for grocery shopping. He texted back that he would pick her up in ten minutes.

Mary took a look in the mirror and brushed her fingers through her hair. She wasn't one for makeup, so it never took her long to get ready. But she did usually like to have a little time to fix her hair before she saw Wes. She did her best, then hurried to the front door to meet him.

"Shh!" Mary put her finger to her lips as she stepped onto the porch with him. "All of the guests are still sleeping."

"Ah, I see." Wes smiled. He bent down to greet Pilot who wagged his tail. They were always excited to see each other. He stood up and took Mary's hand. "I'll be quiet." He closed the door, and guided Mary towards his car.

"Sorry it's not a more adventurous task." Mary settled in the passenger seat.

"Any time with you is worth it to me." Wes looked over at her. "How did things go with Jason, yesterday?"

"He doesn't know too much, yet. But Suzie might have found out the name of the person we found in the mine. He's looking into it." Mary explained who they suspected the skeleton was. She tipped her head towards the grocery store as he pulled in. "I need to be quick. I'd like to be back before the guests wake up."

"I'm at your service." Wes followed her through the front door.

With Wes' help, Mary had her cart full within minutes. She pushed it to the register, which had a few people clustered around it. The moment she walked up, the conversation ceased. Three sets of eyes turned on Mary.

"Good morning." Mary smiled at the cashier as she and Wes put the groceries on the conveyor belt.

"Morning." The cashier began scanning the items but didn't look in Mary's direction.

The two other people lingered by the end of the aisle but remained silent.

"Let me help you bag those up." Wes walked to the end of the aisle and began tossing the items into bags.

"Is it true?" One of the two women at the end of the aisle blurted out.

Mary looked over at her after she handed the cashier the money to pay for the groceries. She didn't recognize her.

"Is what true?"

"Did you and your guests find Jimmy Tomson?" The woman took a step closer to Mary. "His skeleton? In the mine?"

Mary stared back at the woman, as her friend

drew closer. "Where did you hear that?"

"It's all over town." Her friend shrugged. "But no one knows if it's true. Is it really Jimmy Tomson?"

"We did find something, the police are investigating." Mary loaded the bags into the cart, then accepted the change from the cashier. "Forgive me, we're in a bit of a hurry."

"But was it him? Was it Jimmy Tomson?" The younger woman called after her as Mary pushed her cart towards the door.

"Jenny, let it go." The woman's friend put her hand on the woman's shoulder. "You'll find out soon enough."

Mary glanced over her shoulder at Jenny and met her eyes. Was she a friend of Jimmy's? She looked too young to be. Maybe a relative? A wave of guilt made her bite into her bottom lip.

"You did the right thing, Mary." Wes put his hand on her shoulder and guided her through the door. "Jason wouldn't want this spreading around town."

"You're right." Mary was quiet as they loaded the groceries into the trunk, and drove back to Dune House.

"You okay?" Wes looked over at her.

"Someone stole something from the crime scene. I just can't figure out why." Mary gazed at Dune House as he parked. "It looks like no one is up, yet." Maybe the walking group only got up early when they had a hike planned.

"What was taken?" Wes stepped out of the car and began to collect groceries from the trunk.

"A duffel bag. No idea what was in it." Mary grabbed the few remaining bags and followed him into the house.

"I think the key would be to figure out why someone would want to take it in the first place." Wes shrugged as he carried the bags of groceries inside. "My best guess is that there might have been something valuable in there. Either someone took a peek and realized what it was, or someone already knew what was in there."

"Already knew?" Mary raised an eyebrow. "But how could any of them know what was in there? We had all just arrived, and as far as I saw no one looked in the bag."

"Did anyone have a chance, even a second, to be alone with the bag?" Wes handed her a few frozen items.

"Actually, I guess Sam was in there a few seconds before the rest of us went in. He is quite a daring person. He pushed forward the whole time, and yes, he was the first one that went through the door." Mary tucked the frozen items into the freezer, then turned back to Wes for the refrigerated items.

"Then it's possible that he took a peek before anyone else did." Wes set some pantry items on the counter. "Did everyone stay with you on the walk back to Dune House?"

"Actually." Mary winced as she looked away from him. "There is something that I didn't tell Suzie."

"Oh?" Wes set down a box of cereal and looked straight at her. "It's not like you to keep things from her."

"I know." Mary sighed as her cheeks flushed. "I didn't think it was important. I should have told her everything, but at the time, I didn't think it was a big deal, and I just didn't want her to worry. I guess, if I'm telling the truth, I didn't want to admit that I should have listened to her."

"Mary. Whatever it is, it can't be that bad." Wes caught her hand before she could reach for the cereal box. "Suzie cares about you, and so do I. You can tell me anything."

"I guess." Mary frowned, then met his eyes. "I told Suzie that I walked all the way back to Dune

House with the others. But the truth is, I had to stop. I had to take a break. I sent the others ahead with Dalton. But Tiffany stayed back with me. She didn't want me to be alone. I honestly don't know if they all arrived at Dune House together. One of them could have gone off on their own, but now Suzie believes they were all there. What am I going to do?"

"You'll have to tell her." Wes took a breath, then pulled her close. "Don't worry, she'll understand."

"Hi Wes." Suzie stepped into the kitchen. "I didn't expect to see you around this early."

"He helped me with the shopping." Mary turned around to face her with a small smile on her face. "You should know, people are talking about the possibility that it could be Jimmy Tomson in the mine. Two women at the grocery store today mentioned it. I'm not sure how word got out, but it looks like it did."

"Great." Suzie frowned. "I hope it turns out to be the truth, or a lot of people might think they have closure, when they really don't."

"Yes, you're right." Mary glanced over at Wes. "Wes, I can handle the rest of this." She placed a light kiss on his cheek. "I'm sure you have other things to do."

"I do have some errands." Wes glanced between them. "You're sure?" He looked back at Mary.

"Yes, I'm sure. Thanks for your help." Mary turned back to the last bag of groceries.

"See you later, Wes." Suzie took a bag of flour from Mary to put into the pantry. After she heard the door close, she flashed Mary a smile. "He's helping you with errands now? That is pretty serious."

"It was nothing." Mary waved her hand, then cleared her throat. "Suzie, I need to tell you something."

"What is it, Mary?" Suzie focused her attention on her. "Is something wrong?"

"No, but I need to tell you something." Mary gestured to the dining room. "Maybe we could sit?"

"Sure." Suzie followed her into the dining room. "Mary, what's going on, is it the kids?" She sat in the chair that Mary pulled out for her.

"No, the kids are fine, as far as I know." Mary sighed as she looked across the table at her friend. "You know how much I value our friendship, right?"

"Yes, of course I do, Mary." Suzie narrowed her eyes. "What is this about?"

"Yesterday, when I told you that we all walked

back to Dune House together, I had no idea that something had been taken from the mine." Mary frowned. "Otherwise I would have told you the truth."

"The truth? I'm confused. What are you talking about?" Suzie reached across the table and took her hand. "Mary, you can tell me anything."

"I wasn't able to walk back to the house with the others. My knees were killing me. I had to take a break. Only Tiffany stayed with me. I didn't tell you, because I didn't want you to know that I wasn't able to make it." Mary's cheeks reddened. "I'm so sorry, Suzie, I know that you might feel like you can't trust me now."

"Don't be silly, Mary." Suzie stood up from the table and walked around it to hug her. "I'm just sorry that you didn't feel comfortable telling me. I'm sorry if I'm always giving you a hard time about your knees, it's just because I worry about you."

"I understand." Mary took a deep breath and hugged her back. "But now, we don't know who went back to steal that bag."

"That may be true, but we'll figure it out. We always figure it out, right?" Suzie sat down in the chair beside her. "Mary, there's nothing that you could do that would make me not trust you." She frowned. "So, Sam or Dalton or Dawn or Charlie could have gone back into the mine for the bag."

"You know, it's interesting that Charlie is the one that led us to the mine in the first place." Mary shifted in her chair. "We never would have found it, if it wasn't for the paths he chose."

"You're right. But Sam was the first one into the corridor where we found the skeleton." Suzie tipped her head back and forth. "He's a bold guy, and kind of cold, too. Maybe he thought he'd take it for himself to make some kind of profit from it."

"Maybe." Mary narrowed her eyes. "He did have time in the corridor alone to take a peek inside. Then I overheard him and Charlie discussing what to say to Jason before he questioned them."

"Do you think they could have been working together?" Suzie raised an eyebrow. "I hadn't thought about that, but it's possible. Maybe Sam saw what was inside the bag, and told Charlie, and Charlie went back for it?"

"Or maybe Charlie somehow knew it would be there and that is why he led us to the mine." Mary drew a deep breath. "It's so hard to say right now. Hopefully, once the skeleton's identity is confirmed, there will be something that can give us a clue as to why this happened." Mary pulled her phone out of her purse. "Do you remember the employee list we found last night for around the time Jimmy disappeared?"

"Yes, I was going to ask Donald about some of them." Suzie peered at Mary's phone. "Have you found something else?"

"I couldn't sleep last night. I did a search to see if I could find out if any of the employees from the photos still live around here. I think I found the address for one of the employees. It is just outside of Garber, in Parish. I think he might still be local." Mary scrolled to the next screen. "I found what might be a working phone number for him. Should we give him a call? Even if he had nothing to do with the skeleton, he might have some idea of who the skeleton could be, and what happened to get him murdered."

"Yes, absolutely. Give him a call. See if he will meet with us." Suzie glanced up as Dalton descended the last step into the kitchen. "Good morning, Dalton."

"Morning." Dalton walked towards the plate of muffins. "I could definitely eat." He looked over at Suzie. "Any news about our friend in the mine?"

"Nothing yet, I'm afraid." Suzie stood up. "I'll get you some coffee." She walked over to the pot.

"I thought we could do one of the beach hikes today." Dalton checked his watch. "We'd be getting a late start, but maybe it will get everyone's mind off yesterday."

"That's a good idea." Suzie watched Mary as she spoke to someone on the phone, then she handed Dalton a cup of coffee. "Mary and I have some errands to run today, but if you have any trouble, just give either one of us a call, all right?"

"Okay." Dalton looked towards Mary. "Is she doing all right? It seemed like she was in a lot of pain yesterday."

"Yes, she was." Suzie frowned. "She mentioned that she had to rest while you led the others back here. Did they all stay with you?"

"Actually, no. Just Dawn and I stuck together. Charlie and Sam found another path they wanted to check out. But we all ended up back here, eventually." Dalton took a bite of his muffin, then smiled as Dawn entered the kitchen. "Good morning, Dawn. You have to try one of these muffins."

"Coffee," Dawn mumbled as she leaned against the counter. "Coffee, before anything."

"Coming right up." Suzie grinned.

CHAPTER 8

*M*ary ended the call, as Suzie joined her at the table again.

"Did you get a hold of him?" Suzie peeked at the notes that Mary had jotted down on a napkin.

"Yes, his name is Scott Alguin and he agreed to meet with us at the diner for lunch." Mary looked up at her with a smile. "I hope you don't mind that I went ahead and set up a meeting. I didn't want us to miss the opportunity."

"Not at all. That reminds me. I should call Paul and see how his meeting went yesterday. You know, I bet he doesn't know anything about any of this. I haven't even texted him." Suzie pulled out her phone.

CINDY BELL

"Really Suzie?" Mary raised an eyebrow. "You didn't want to tell him right away?"

"I guess I just got caught up in the investigation and didn't really think about it." Suzie grabbed her keys and headed for the door. "I'll just give him a call on the way to see Donald. When I come back, we can head out to the diner."

"Sounds good." Mary greeted Tiffany as she entered the kitchen. "Good morning, Tiffany."

"Morning." Tiffany yawned, then smiled at Dawn and Dalton. "I see you two are already getting your caffeine. Any plans for today?"

"A beach trail." Dawn nodded. "Dalton thinks it will be a good change of pace."

"Let's hope we don't find any sunken pirate ships." Tiffany picked up a muffin.

"At least there might be treasure." Charlie joked, as he joined them in the kitchen.

"Where is Sam this morning?" Mary stepped into the kitchen to pour coffee and start a new pot.

"Oh, he's around here somewhere, I imagine." Charlie smiled as he took his cup of coffee. "Thanks for this."

"He probably already went out for a run on the beach. He's an early riser." Dalton pointed through the kitchen window. "There he is now."

92

Mary's eyes widened as she watched Sam jog towards the porch. She had no idea that he had been up. Had he heard anything that she and Wes had discussed? Or what she and Suzie had discovered?

"Let's go out on the porch with him." Dalton picked up his coffee and muffin. Soon the entire group had assembled on the porch, which gave Mary the chance to take a deep breath. If Sam had overheard their conversation, he wasn't acting like it. He joked and smiled with the others. In fact, as Mary observed, he seemed to be happier than she had seen him since he arrived. What was putting him in such a good mood?

Mary cleaned the kitchen as she waited for Suzie to return so they could go to the diner. Mary was lost in thought wiping down the counter, when Suzie came in through the door.

"Hi Mary." Suzie put her purse on the counter.

"How did the visit go?" Mary asked.

"It didn't." Suzie rolled her eyes. "I drove all the way there only to be turned away by his receptionist. She said that he wasn't even taking any appointments."

"I'm sorry." Mary frowned.

"We should head to the diner." Mary added

some more fruit to the bowl, then grabbed her purse. "How is Paul?"

"Honestly?" Suzie cringed. "He was a little annoyed that I didn't call him yesterday. But now that he's filled in, he mentioned that the man who he met with yesterday is actually Donald's son. He was so insistent about meeting with Paul the same night he docked, but Paul refused. When Paul spoke with him at breakfast the next day, Bob tried to get him to agree to a contract with him for whale watching tours. When Paul refused, Bob got pretty annoyed and left without finishing his food." She shook her head. "The whole thing seems odd to me." She led Mary through the door to the parking lot.

"That is strange. It sounds like Bob is pretty desperate." Mary opened the passenger side door. "Maybe that's why the mine is up for sale. Maybe Bob and Donald are having financial trouble and need to get some kind of cash for the property."

"Could be." Suzie turned on the car and started the short journey towards the diner. "I would have loved to speak to Donald today. I tried to get an appointment with him, but apparently, he doesn't speak to anyone directly anymore. His son deals with all of that. I'll see if Paul can arrange an appointment for me to speak with Donald tomorrow. He might have more pull than me. I did manage to get an appointment with Bob later in the week in case Paul can't get me in to see Donald."

"How did you manage that?" Mary raised an eyebrow as she looked over at her.

"I just convinced the receptionist that I was a local business owner that wanted to discuss an idea with him." Suzie turned into the diner. "It wasn't exactly a lie. At least, not all of it."

"True." Mary joined her as she walked towards the door of the diner. "If Donald was the owner at the time of Jimmy's murder, I wonder if he ever even considered looking in the mine for him."

"I don't think anyone would have. It was shut down, there shouldn't have been anyone inside." Suzie held open the door for her.

"Someone was. Two people at least. I doubt it could just be some random person. It was probably someone that knew the mine well enough to find their way back out of that maze." Mary scanned the gathering of patrons. Lunch was always a busy time at the diner. It was a popular place to eat thanks to the good food and friendly service. "There he is, Suzie." She pointed to a man who sat alone at a table. He looked to be in his sixties, and already had a plate with the diner's famous chicken sandwich and fries in front of him. Mary led the way to the table. "Scott?"

"I'm Scott." He looked up at her and smiled. "You must be Mary."

"I am, and this is my friend Suzie. Can we join you?" Mary reached for one of the chairs.

"Sure." Scott pulled his plate back a bit to give them some room. "But like I said on the phone, I'm not sure how much I can tell you. That was a long time ago."

Mary noticed some dirt smudges on Scott's hands as he picked up his sandwich.

"We don't need to know much." Suzie sat down across from him. "We just need you to be our eyes and ears for those final days before the mine closed. Did Jimmy have any arguments with anyone in particular? Had he been acting strangely?"

"Jimmy was always kind of a strange guy. He was always up to something." Scott took another bite.

"It must have upset you when he fired you." Mary locked her eyes to his. "Were other people upset, too?"

"Look, if you want to know who had a bone to pick with Jimmy Tomson, it was a guy called Charlie." Scott paused to chew his bite of food, then continued. "As far as I'm concerned, Jimmy did me a favor." He wiped some crumbs from his lips with the back of his hand. "He let me go, and just a few days later the mine shut down. Thanks to him I was able to get back on my feet a lot faster than the rest of the guys that got blindsided with the shutdown. I had no reason to cause him any harm."

"Surely you were upset, though?" Suzie leaned forward. "Did you two have a fight? Is that why he fired you?"

"We exchanged words. He accused me of stealing." Scott rolled his eyes. "As if I could ever get a single gold nugget out of that place without someone catching me. He searched us all on our way out, every day. We had to turn in our gear before we were allowed to leave the mine. He had no proof that I stole anything, but he accused me just the same."

"Who is Charlie? How do you know he had a problem with Jimmy?" Mary shifted the focus of the conversation as she sensed that he didn't harbor animosity towards Jimmy. It sounded like Jimmy was a paranoid boss, and perhaps with good reason.

"He arrived out of the blue, shortly before the mine closed, he stayed here for a few days and he confronted Jimmy. They had a huge argument about something, I'm not sure what though."

"Do you know what Charlie looked like?" Mary asked.

"Sure, he looked well—" Scott cleared his throat, then closed his eyes and tipped his head from side to side. "He was pretty average to be honest." When he opened his eyes again, they widened. He pointed past her, towards the front door of the diner. "He looked a lot like that, only younger."

Mary turned her head in time to see Charlie head for one of the empty tables. Her heart skipped a beat. Could Charlie be the same man that Jimmy had a problem with?

"Are you sure about that?" Suzie stood up from her chair.

"Sure as I can be, more than twenty years later." Scott tilted his head back and waved. "Hey Charlie!"

Charlie turned towards their table, then froze.

"Charlie, it's me, Scott." Scott stood up from the table. "We played cards together a couple of times, remember? Your son played a couple of games of basketball with the team that I coached. You must remember?"

"Sorry, no." Charlie backed out through the door of the diner.

"I'm going after him." Suzie ran towards the door. "Charlie, wait!" She caught up with him in the parking lot of the diner.

"Suzie, I was just going to grab a sandwich." Charlie shrugged. "Now that I see how busy it is, I decided against it."

"You didn't go hiking with the others?" Suzie fell into step beside him.

"I didn't feel up to it. After yesterday, I'm a little worn out. In case you haven't noticed, I'm not as young as the rest of them." Charlie rubbed a hand along the back of his neck. "I need a little recovery time."

"You seemed to be keeping up just fine yesterday. You even led the way most of the time." Suzie paused beside him as he reached the edge of the parking lot and stopped.

"Yes well, the first day is always easy enough. But waking up after it is rough." Charlie glanced back at the diner. "Sorry, if I was rude to your friend in there. He obviously mistook me for someone else."

"He's not my friend. I just met him." Suzie

studied his expression. "He used to work at the mine, shortly before it closed."

"Is that so?" Charlie cleared his throat. "And he thought he knew me?"

"He recalled you being around the mine at that time." Suzie's muscles tightened as she decided to take the plunge and watch Charlie's reaction. "Did you know a man named Jimmy Tomson?"

"Is that who was in the corridor?" Charlie's eyes suddenly locked to hers.

"Did you know him?" Suzie pressed, her gaze stern.

"Have they identified him?" Charlie's knees bent. He reached for a nearby bench to steady himself.

"Not officially. Have you been to Garber before, Charlie?" Suzie guided him to sit down on the bench. Then she sat down beside him.

"I might have been, sure." Charlie sat forward and rested his elbows on his knees. "But I never lived here."

"You just came here to confront Jimmy Tomson? Why?" Suzie leaned closer to him.

"That's nonsense. I have no idea what you're talking about." Charlie gritted his teeth.

"I think you do. I think that's why you wouldn't

talk to Scott in there." Suzie frowned. "Charlie, it's going to come out sooner or later. You can't just deny your way out of this."

"I knew I never should have come here." Charlie pressed his hands over his face and began to rock back and forth. "I told myself not to go on this trip, that it would stir up old memories. But here I am. Now, I'm stuck in the middle of all of this nonsense."

"You don't have to be stuck, if you just tell the truth." Suzie clasped her hands together. "Did you have a problem with Jimmy back then?"

"I don't have to be stuck?" Charlie stood up from the bench and stared at her. "Are you kidding me? If that's Jimmy Tomson in that mine, then I am as good as done for. I came here to have a nice outing, with a group of people that I consider to be friends. I did not come here to dredge up my past, or to get stuck in the middle of this town's murder mystery." He shook his head. "I have nothing more to say about this."

As Charlie stalked off, Suzie stared after him. It was clear to her that he was hiding something, and that he had been in Garber around the time of Jimmy's disappearance. Armed with this information, she knew she had to get it to Jason as soon as possible.

"Suzie, did you talk to him?" Mary joined her at the edge of the parking lot.

"I did." Suzie filled her in on the conversation. "I'm going to go talk to Jason about it."

"Take the car. I'll walk home." Mary nodded. "Jason needs to know this information and I would like the walk."

"Okay, call me if you need me." Suzie thought about objecting but decided against it. She gave her a quick hug. Then she ducked back into the diner for a take-out order. She knew better than to deliver Jason any kind of news on an empty stomach.

As Suzie drove to the police station she wondered if Jason would see things the way she did. Charlie seemed like a nice enough man, but she really knew nothing about him. If he had killed Jimmy Tomson, and then wanted the remains to be discovered for some reason, that meant that he had planned out the entire event. It left her unsettled to think that she had unwittingly participated in his hoax. But what if he was innocent? What if he had nothing to do with Jimmy's death, or the discovery of Jimmy's skeleton?

As Suzie pulled into the parking lot of the police

station, she noticed Dalton near the entrance. Dawn stood beside him with her arm wrapped around his shoulders and his arm around her waist. Alarmed, Suzie parked her car, then walked up to them.

"Dalton, Dawn, is everything okay?"

"It's fine." Dalton pulled Dawn a little closer. "We just had a little scare on the beach is all."

"What kind of scare?" Suzie looked Dawn over. "Are you hurt?"

"No, I'm fine." Dawn frowned. "So far, this trip isn't going well, though. We were walking on the beach, and then all of a sudden, this woman came out of nowhere. She started shouting at all of us. She demanded to see Charlie, but I had no idea who she was."

"We didn't tell her anything." Dalton met Suzie's eyes. "I don't know what's going on, but Charlie seems like a stand up guy."

"Do you know him well?" Suzie recalled the way Charlie had reacted to Scott's presence. He'd wanted to get out of there as fast as he could. Did he have something more to hide?

"Not at all, actually. This is his first time hiking with us. He suggested we come to Garber. He said he wanted a change of pace. So, we let him join in."

Dalton narrowed his eyes. "He told me about the secret waterfall."

"He did." Suzie's eyes widened.

"This woman on the beach, she kept shouting that she had to see Charlie. It frightened Dawn so much that she twisted her ankle when she turned to walk away. Sam told her to get lost, and Tiffany threatened to call the police. I thought we should follow through and report it. Now we're headed back to Dune House."

"We might stop and sit on the beach on the way." Dawn nodded. "Sitting with my toes in the sand watching the sea always helps me relax."

"That sounds like a good idea. Mary should be at Dune House, if you need anything. How is your ankle, Dawn?" Suzie looked down at Dawn's feet.

"It's all right. It wasn't as bad as I thought. I was more scared than anything. I thought this was a quiet place." Dawn clutched Dalton's arm. "I've never seen anyone behave like that."

"Did you catch her name?" Suzie pulled out her phone.

"No, I didn't. But I'd sure know her if I saw her again." Dawn shivered.

"Let's get you back to the house." Dalton looked over his shoulder at Suzie. "I'm not sure that we'll be staying much longer. I know that none of this is your fault, but at this point, I don't think anyone is having any fun."

Suzie watched them walk away. It would be a blow if they left early, or left a bad review about their stay, but if they took the missing bag with them, that would be even worse. She had to work fast to help find out what really happened in that mine, both when Jimmy died, and when the bag went missing.

CHAPTER 9

*S*uzie pulled open the door to the police station and stepped inside. It was fairly quiet, despite the crowd of people that had clustered around the front desk. She caught the eye of a familiar officer, and he tipped his head towards the hallway that led to Jason's office. She smiled, then continued down it. When she reached Jason's office, she found his door open and Jason hunched over a pile of files on his desk. As she expected, he was hard at work on the case. She knocked lightly on the frame of the door.

"Jason?"

"Suzie?" He looked up at her and smiled. "Come in. Sit."

Suzie smiled back as she sat down in the chair across from Jason's desk.

"I'm sorry to just drop in like this, but it seemed easier than texting or calling." Suzie offered him the bag from the diner.

"It's no problem. I was due for a breather." Jason accepted the take-out bag from her. "Oh, and that smells so good."

"I thought you might like it." Suzie smiled. "I know how you are when you're working a case. You forget to eat."

"Summer is always on me about it." Jason rubbed the heel of his palm into his forehead, just above his eye. "I get headaches sometimes. But right now, she's too busy to remind me. She's confirmed the skeleton's identity, and now is trying to estimate when he died." He looked across the desk at her. "You were right. It is Jimmy Tomson."

"You're sure?" Suzie's eyes widened.

"Yes, it's been confirmed by dental records." Jason took a bite of his sandwich.

"Well, that's a step in the right direction." Suzie frowned. "Why wasn't he ever reported as missing?"

"He lived with his brother at the time, Carter. I spoke with him a little while ago. Carter claimed that he and Jimmy got into a fight and Jimmy said he was leaving town. So, when he disappeared, he just assumed that was what happened." Jason set his sandwich down. "But like you mentioned, there were many people around town that didn't believe Jimmy would just disappear like that. It turns out, he didn't. Summer found another bullet wound in his back. She can't confirm it yet, but she says he was most likely dead for about the length of time the mine has been closed."

"Wow, I suspected it, but now that I know for sure, it's still surprising. He managed the employees of that mine, and then not long after it closed, he lost his life there?" Suzie rested her elbows on his desk. "Did Carter have anything else to say?"

"It turns out Charlie Hume, the same Charlie that is staying at Dune House, and Jimmy went to high school together in Bernard." Jason rocked back in his chair and folded his hands behind his head. "Jimmy and Charlie's wife, Sarah, were quite a thing in high school. But when they all graduated, Charlie ended up with her. He married her. Jimmy moved on."

"Or didn't." Suzie snapped her fingers. "An ex-employee of the mine I spoke to today, Scott Alguin, said that he saw Charlie around Jimmy, and that they had a fight, not long before he disappeared.

Maybe there were some rumors that Jimmy and Sarah had rekindled an affair. Maybe Charlie decided that he'd had enough and wanted things to be over between his wife and Jimmy once and for all." She gritted her teeth as she recalled the conversation she had with Charlie. He certainly hadn't told her the whole story.

"Maybe." Jason picked up his sandwich again. "But, we're a long way off from being able to prove that. I'll talk to him again, though."

"Good idea. The thing is, even if he did kill Jimmy so long ago, that still wouldn't explain why he would come back here, why he would lead us to the mine."

"Maybe he just decided it was time that Jimmy was found." Jason finished the last bite of his sandwich. "Sometimes people just can't live with a secret any longer."

"Maybe." Suzie closed her eyes and did her best to recall the moment that Charlie found the door. "He certainly did lead the way. But there were much easier ways for Jimmy's body to be found. Maybe somehow, he knew about the bag, and he wanted to get it back. If only we knew what was inside of it, we might be able to get an idea of who took it."

"I think we might have an idea of what it was."

Jason flipped open a file on his desk. "Crime scene techs found some tiny shavings of gold on the floor around where I'm guessing the bag was." He pointed to the empty space in the picture. "There wasn't as much dust or grime built up in this area, and it looks about the size of a duffel bag."

"Gold shavings?" Suzie's heart skipped a beat. "Are you saying that you think it was a bag full of gold?"

"At least some." Jason nodded. "That would be pretty good motivation for someone to steal it. Obviously, I can't know for sure what was in it, but that is the theory I am running with right now. I imagine it would have been quite heavy."

"Gold," Suzie repeated, and sat back in her chair. "This changes everything."

"It does?" Jason eyed her. "What do you mean?"

"I mean, maybe no one went into that mine intending to find Jimmy Tomson. Maybe someone went into that mine looking for the bag of gold, and just happened upon his remains." Suzie scooted her chair closer to his desk. "Just because Jimmy had an affair with Charlie's wife, that doesn't mean that Charlie killed him. Maybe he knew about the bag of gold and suspected that it was still hidden somewhere in the mine."

111

"It's possible. But it's a stretch. Right now, all of the evidence is pointing right at Charlie." Jason brushed some crumbs from his hands. "The problem is, I don't have any actual evidence. Yes, Charlie was in the mine, but he was there with the rest of you. We have no way to prove that he returned to the mine to get the bag. Nor do I have any physical evidence to link him to Jimmy's murder. Although, that could change as results continue to come in."

"Scott's local, and Jimmy fired him not long before he died," Suzie explained. "He accused Scott of stealing. Maybe Scott decided he knew too much, and he had to get rid of him. Or maybe Jimmy caught him with the bag of gold and confronted him."

"Maybe. But the part I don't understand is, why would anyone kill Jimmy, but leave the gold behind?" Jason met her eyes across his desk. "If there was gold in that bag like I think, it could be worth quite a bit. So why leave it behind?"

"Maybe the killer worried that taking it would implicate them in Jimmy's murder?" Suzie stood up. "I know you have a lot of work to do. I'll let you get back to it."

"Suzie, there's one other thing." Jason stood up as

well. "The owners of the mine, Donald and Terrance, they have both retained lawyers. I'm guessing they are expecting criminal charges or a lawsuit for not keeping the mine inaccessible. I have been trying to reach Terrance but have not been able to. He is still out of the country, but Donald and his son Bob aren't. I just want you to be cautious. At this time, we have no idea who Jimmy's killer could be. Charlie is a good bet, but there are some flaws in that theory. Too many to give up on any other suspects at this point."

"I'll be careful, Jason." Suzie smiled. "And you make sure you eat."

As Suzie left the police station, she already had her phone in her hand. She was not going to wait any longer to meet with Donald.

"Hi Paul." She smiled at the sound of his voice. "I need you to do me a favor, please."

When Mary returned to Dune House, she found Tiffany in the living room. Despite the wide selection of comfortable furniture, she paced back and forth across the room.

"Tiffany?" Mary set down her purse on the

coffee table and walked over to the woman. "Are you okay?"

"There are some weird people in this town." Tiffany crossed her arms as she looked at Mary. "I thought small towns were quaint, but you really have your crazies, don't you?"

"What happened?" Mary sat down on the couch and gestured for Tiffany to sit beside her. "I thought you went out for a hike on the beach."

"We did, and we ran into this woman that shouted at us. She wanted to see Charlie, and when we told her that we didn't know where he was, she continued to shout and demand to see him. It was scary." Tiffany clasped her hands together in her lap. "Dalton and Dawn went to the police station to report it, because the woman seemed so unhinged."

"Did she say what her name was?" Mary scooted closer to her and wrapped an arm around her shoulders. "I'm sorry that you had to experience that."

"She didn't tell us her name, but someone shouted it from the dock. I think it was Jenny. I can't be sure, though." Tiffany shook her head. "It was a woman on the dock that was shouting at her."

"Jenny." Mary's eyes narrowed. She recalled the woman in the grocery store earlier that day. Could it be the same person? "Did she say anything about why she was looking for him?"

"No, she just kept demanding to see him." Tiffany sighed. "I have no idea where Charlie is. I'm worried that she's going to show up here looking for him."

"Did you feel threatened by her?" Mary grabbed her purse from the coffee table and rummaged in it for her phone.

"Not exactly. She just seemed so upset, and determined. No matter how many times we told her that he wasn't with us, she wouldn't believe us." Tiffany sighed and wiped a hand across her forehead. "I don't know what Charlie got himself into, but whatever it is, it doesn't sound good."

"Do you know him well?" Mary opened the notepad on her phone and began to type out a few notes about what Tiffany said.

"I've never met him before this trip. It's the first one he's come with us on." Tiffany frowned and folded her hands in her lap. "He seemed nice enough."

"Have you hiked with the others before?" Mary leaned closer. "Sam?"

"Yes, Sam, Dalton, and Dawn. We've been hiking together for over a year. No one thought adding Charlie to the mix would be an issue." Tiffany stood up and began to pace, again. "I guess we should have found out a little more about him."

Mary pursed her lips. After what Scott had to say about Charlie being around when Jimmy disappeared, she tended to agree with Tiffany. But she didn't want to give too much away. She had already heard Sam and Charlie whispering to each other, which meant that Sam might be part of whatever Charlie was up to. But it also meant that other members of the hiking group could be involved as well.

"Dalton seems to be in charge most of the time. Is that how it usually is?"

"He finds the places for us to hike, we can make suggestions, like Charlie suggested this place, but yes, I guess Dalton's opinion carries more weight. He and Dawn work together, and Dawn is my neighbor. Sam is a friend of Dalton's from college." Tiffany ran her hands along her thighs and took a deep breath. "I've got to calm down. I tend to get anxious about things. I'm working on it."

"It's okay, we all feel that way sometimes." Mary pushed herself up to her feet. "Listen Tiffany, I know all of this has been a lot for you to handle. I'm sorry that it's happened. I really wanted you all to enjoy your stay here at Dune House."

"I know none of this is your fault, Mary, but it's hard to relax and enjoy such a beautiful place, when strange things are happening. I still have no idea who deleted those pictures off my phone. I think the police suspect me of something because the pictures have gone missing." Tiffany crossed her arms. "But I honestly didn't delete them."

"I believe you. I know you didn't, Tiffany." Mary set her phone down and focused her attention on the woman across from her. "I just want to make sure that you know you don't have to worry. Suzie and I will make sure that no one disturbs you here. No one besides the guests will have access to Dune House. I'll make us all a nice dinner tonight, and we can have a fire in the fireplace. It'll be a peaceful evening."

"That sounds absolutely wonderful." Tiffany released a heavy sigh. "Thanks Mary. I think I'm going to go lie down for a bit."

"Good idea." Mary smiled as she watched her walk out of the living room. Her smile faded once she was alone. It seemed to her that Charlie was a big part of all of this. Was it safe to have him in Dune House? She didn't think so. After overhearing his conversation with Sam, she was more than a little suspicious of him. After the scene at the diner, and Scott's identification of Charlie as someone that Jimmy had a problem with, she was even more concerned. She picked up her phone again and dialed Wes' number. He answered on the first ring.

"Mary, how are you doing?"

"I'm okay, thanks. I'm wondering if you can do me a favor. I don't want to take advantage of you, so if you don't want to do it, please understand that I'm just fine with that." Mary began to pace back and forth across the living room.

"Just tell me what it is. I'm sure that I can help you with anything you need."

"Thanks Wes." Mary smiled at the warmth in his voice. "Do you think you could do a background check on Charlie for me?"

"Charlie, sure." Wes paused, then continued. "Is there anything you want to tell me?"

"I just have an uneasy feeling about him at this point." Mary explained what they had learned from Scott and about the women looking for Charlie. "It would put me at ease to know that he has a clean record."

"I can check that for you right now. Hold on a second."

Mary perched on the arm of the couch and waited. The clicking sound of keys being pressed carried over the phone.

"Eh, I can go a little deeper, but the initial results are that he doesn't have a single thing on his record."

"Nothing?" Mary raised an eyebrow. She had expected at least a misdemeanor of some kind.

"Nothing. If he's ever been in any kind of trouble, there's nothing on record. It does show that he was married to Sarah Coopers, though." Wes cleared his throat. "Does that help anything?"

"Wait, did you say, was married? As in they aren't married anymore?" Mary focused her attention on his response.

"Yes, was. The divorce took place not long after the mine closed."

"Interesting. I wonder what caused them to split." Mary bit into her bottom lip.

"Sometimes couples just don't last, I'd guess they just stopped getting along. There are so many things that can strain a relationship."

"Yes, that's possible. What about any children?" Mary had never asked Charlie if he had kids. In fact, she hadn't asked much about him at all.

"Charlie has a son from a previous relationship and Sarah had one child, Jennifer Coopers."

"Jenny." Mary narrowed her eyes. "So, it was her in the store, and her on the beach."

"It could have been. Or it could have been someone else named Jenny. I don't think that's likely, though. It sounds like Charlie's past is catching up with him in more ways than one."

"Yes, it does. Thanks Wes." As Mary ended the call she wondered if Charlie had known that coming back to Garber would stir so much up for him. She guessed that he must have suspected. Which made her believe that he knew about the gold. Why else would a reasonable person step back into a hornet's nest? He must have thought the reward would be worth the nuisance. Now she wondered if he still felt the same way.

CHAPTER 10

"Suzie, are you sure about this?" Paul caught her arm just before she could pull open the door of the office. He met her eyes, his own narrowed. "This isn't a simple matter, if Donald really was involved. He might suspect why you are really here, why I set up this meeting with his son and insisted that he be there."

"Yes, I'm sure. I need to find out as much as I can about this situation as fast as I can. It's okay if they suspect. I'm no threat to him. I'm not the police, I'm not anyone but an interested business person." Suzie gazed back at him. "Trust me, Paul, I can handle anything that they throw at me."

"It's not you that I don't trust." Paul pulled open

the door, then passed one more look in her direction. "I'll follow your lead."

Suzie stepped inside and walked past the empty reception desk. She continued down the hall to the only door, which stood ajar.

"Paul?" Bob stepped into the doorway. "Come in." He stepped back as Suzie approached. "Oh, I didn't know that we'd have company."

"Is your father here?" Suzie continued on into the office and noticed an older man seated behind the desk. "Donald?"

"That's me." Donald stood up from his chair and offered his hand to Suzie. "And you are?"

"My name is Suzie." She shook his hand and smiled at him. "Thanks for agreeing to this meeting."

"When I agreed to this meeting, it was with Paul." Donald's gaze passed over his son and settled on Paul. "Somehow, I think this meeting isn't about a business deal between us."

"I did call the meeting to discuss something." Paul held out his hand towards Suzie. "At her request."

"What is this nonsense?" Bob frowned as he looked between both of them. "I came here to make a deal."

"I came here to ask you a few questions. I hope you don't mind." Suzie sat down in a chair in front of the desk. "I'm not sure if you have heard the rumors."

"About Jimmy Tomson?" Donald lifted his chin, then nodded. "I've heard them."

"She's the one that owns Dune House, Dad." Bob leaned against the desk not far from Suzie's chair. "You're the one that found Jimmy, aren't you?"

"Not just me, but yes." Suzie sat forward in her chair as Paul stepped up beside her. "I'm very sorry for your loss. I'm sure that you didn't expect this." She locked her eyes to Donald's.

"I didn't expect that he would be in the mine, no." Donald narrowed his eyes. "But I knew it would only be a matter of time before he got himself into some kind of trouble."

"You did?" Suzie raised an eyebrow. "What made you think that?"

"He was always on someone's bad side. If it wasn't the workers, it was someone else." Donald shook his head, then folded his hands on top of the desk. "He was a good worker, I'm not saying that he wasn't, but he got people riled up very easily. I had to show up there once when the workers threatened to revolt if he wasn't fired. He was such a stickler for the rules."

"That sounds terrible." Suzie glanced over at Bob, whose eyes remained on her. Then she looked back at Donald. "So, you two weren't close?"

"We would throw back a few beers now and then. We'd meet up to discuss the mine, and improvements we could make. But we weren't close on a personal level." Donald peered at her. "What is this all about anyway? Why do you need to know any of this?"

"Honestly, I don't. I didn't know Jimmy. I'm fairly new to Garber, actually. But I am a business owner, and the most important part of my business is that people have to trust that the location they visit is safe, and that the adventures they have will not be traumatic. Right now, I'm staring down the barrel of some very bad reviews. I thought if I could at least give my guests a few more details about what happened, they might feel reassured enough not to cut their vacation short. I'm sure you can understand that it doesn't take much to threaten the health of a business."

"Yes, I can certainly understand that." Donald tapped his hand lightly against the desk. "Of course, the mine is closed, and none of you had any right to be in it. In fact, I could be pressing charges right now for trespassing."

"That wouldn't be wise." Paul placed his hand on Suzie's shoulder as he stared at Donald.

"It wouldn't, would it?" Donald smiled as he looked up at Paul. "Which is why I'm not doing it. I shouldn't even be having this conversation with you, Suzie because I am at risk of a lawsuit by you and your guests. According to my lawyers, the mine should have been boarded up completely to prevent access. So you see, I'm in a poor position here, too."

"I don't think you have anything to worry about. I know you don't have anything to worry about from me. I know we took a risk when we stepped into that mine." Suzie looked into his eyes. "If you're willing to help me with my problem, by telling me a little more about the mine, and about Jimmy Tomson, then I'd be willing to try to persuade my guests not to even consider a lawsuit."

"I like the way you think." Donald grinned. He looked up at Paul. "You should keep her around. She'll keep you out of trouble."

"I intend to." Paul's hand tightened some on Suzie's shoulder.

"So, what do you want to know?" Donald turned his attention back to Suzie.

"When did you last see Jimmy Tomson? Did you meet up with him after the mine closed?" Suzie slipped her hand into her pocket and turned the audio recorder on her phone to on. She couldn't trust herself to remember every detail.

"After the mine closed, we were done. I never spoke to him again." Donald shrugged. "Not long after, I heard rumors that he took off. Apparently, there was some trouble with the husband of a girl he was seeing." He smirked. "Like I said, he liked to live dangerously."

"I see. And what about your partner, Terrance? Did he have any contact with Jimmy?" Suzie noticed Bob's attention snap to his father.

"Terrance was a silent partner. He helped me out with the original investment, and filtered money in here and there when needed. But the day to day operation of the mine, he left to me. He didn't live in the country. He only visited a few times. I highly doubt that he ever had any contact with Jimmy." Donald smoothed his gray hair back behind his ear. "That was so long ago."

"But you recently put the land and mine up for sale. Why is that?" Suzie glanced at Bob, and saw his jaw rippled with tension.

"It's a dead weight. We're ready to unload it." Donald shrugged. "Nothing more to it than that."

"What about the husband that Jimmy had trouble with? Or any particular employee that had a problem with him?" Suzie noted that Bob began to relax, just before he spoke up.

"There was one guy that hated Jimmy. Scott was his name. I remember the two of them getting into a fist fight once. Remember that, Dad?" Bob looked over at him. "I was just a kid at the time."

"Yes, I remember. Jimmy rubbed Scott up the wrong way. Jimmy wanted to fire him, but I wouldn't let him, at first. Scott's family and my family were from around the same parts, Scott coached the basketball team Bob played for as well, and I promised his father that Scott would always have a job as long as the mine was open. Eventually, I let Jimmy fire him though, when he was suspected of stealing. As for the husband, I think his name was Charlie. His son and Bob played basketball a couple of times together. But that's all I know about that." Donald took a breath then looked straight at Suzie. "I hope I can count on your help to make this troubling matter become a little less trouble."

"You can." Suzie stood up and offered him her

hand. As he shook it, she smiled. "Thanks for your time, Donald."

"Paul, I'd still like to talk to you about that business opportunity." Bob stepped between them and the door.

"Not today, Bob. But I'll keep it in mind." Paul gestured for Suzie to walk out the door in front of him.

As soon as Mary heard the front door knob turn, she jumped to her feet. The door wasn't usually locked, but she had locked it, just as she promised Tiffany she would. All of the guests had keys to the house as the doors were locked overnight. There was a good chance the person at the door was Suzie, or Jason, but there was also a chance that it was Charlie. Was she ready to look him in the eye?

By the time Mary reached the foyer, the knob had turned all the way and the door swung open.

"Mary?" Suzie froze in the doorway as she locked eyes with her friend. "What's going on? Why was the door locked?"

"Suzie, we have a serious problem. Charlie's

daughter and I believe his ex-wife are in Garber, and looking for him." Mary rushed past her and locked the door. "Jenny, Charlie's daughter, confronted Dalton, Dawn, Sam, and Tiffany, when they were walking on the beach. She wouldn't leave them alone."

"I knew they had a run-in with someone on the beach. I ran into Dalton and Dawn at the police station after they reported it. I didn't know that it was Charlie's daughter, though. Are you sure about that?" Suzie frowned. "Do you really think it's necessary to lock the door?"

"Yes, absolutely. Tiffany is upstairs resting, but she was so upset the poor girl was shaking. I promised her that no one besides the guests would be able to get in here." Mary rubbed her hands together as she drew a slow breath. "All of this has me feeling pretty anxious, Suzie. What are we going to do about Charlie?"

"What do you mean?" Suzie led Mary into the living room.

"I mean, if he is caught up in this dispute with his ex-wife and child, and also possibly involved in some way with the murder of Jimmy Tomson, is it safe to have him in Dune House with the other guests, and us?" Mary glanced through the living room window that overlooked part of the parking lot and the woods beyond it.

"I'm not sure what we can do." Suzie clasped her hands behind her back as she paced. "At this time, he hasn't been charged with anything. We don't have any proof that he was involved in any of this. We can't exactly just throw him out."

"I know, but I wish we could." Mary turned back to face her. "You didn't see how upset Tiffany was. Plus, we know that he was most likely the one who took the gold. Which means he's been lying to us. He led us into that mine." She took a sharp breath. "I'm sorry, I know this isn't like me, but it bothers me that he has lied to us. We certainly can't trust him."

"After the conversation I just had with Donald, I'd say there are many people that we can't trust. It seems that many of those people have skeletons in their closets." Suzie sat down on the edge of the couch and gazed at the palms of her hands as she filled Mary in on what she learned from her meeting with Donald and Bob. "Okay. Let's talk to Charlie first." Suzie stood up from the couch again. "He's not the only one that had a bone to pick with Jimmy. Scott isn't telling us the whole story about his interaction with Jimmy, either. I just want to take things one step at a time if possible." She met Mary's eyes. "So, we'll see how Charlie reacts when we mention that his ex and his daughter were looking for him, and we'll take it from there."

"Okay." Mary frowned. "But I don't feel good about any of this."

"Me either." Suzie patted Mary's shoulder and gazed at her friend. "We're going to get through this. But we have to be smart about it. If we throw Charlie out without a valid reason, word could get around, and people will not want to stay here. We have a business to think of, too."

"Yes, you're right." Mary wrung her hands. She jumped as the front door opened, then she looked at Suzie.

Suzie stepped out into the hallway, just as Charlie closed the door behind him.

"Charlie." Suzie called out as he stepped farther inside. Mary joined her in the hallway.

"Yes?" Charlie looked between them, his eyes wide.

"I would like to talk if you have a second." Suzie gestured to the living room, while blocking his path any farther into the house.

"I'd really rather not." Charlie's brow wrinkled

as he took a step forward. "I've been having a rough day."

"That's what we would like to talk about." Mary's voice softened as she spoke. "We just need to clear a few things up."

"There's nothing I want to discuss." Charlie straightened his shoulders. "Now, if you wouldn't mind, I'd like to go to my room."

"That's the problem." Suzie continued to block his way. "We need to be sure that the rest of the guests in this house are not put at risk by your presence."

"Excuse me?" Charlie chuckled. "You have quite the imagination, don't you?"

"I don't think it's my imagination that your ex-wife and daughter were demanding to speak with you." Suzie narrowed her eyes as she studied him. "Your daughter was quite insistent and would not leave the others alone."

"My daughter?" Charlie rolled his eyes. "You don't have your story straight. I have every right to be here."

"Perhaps I'm mistaken, but I'm not mistaken about the fact that she was looking for you." Suzie took a deep breath. "Charlie, we're not trying to give you a hard time, we're just trying to figure out what's going on here."

"Yes, we're just as concerned about your well-being." Mary met his eyes. "She left everyone quite shaken. Which means that she must have been quite upset when she spoke with them. Clearly she wants an audience with you."

"She is the one stalking me, and I am the one who is the danger?" Charlie looked between them, drew a slow breath, then exhaled. "Look ladies, I've had a lot of things happen to me in life. My marriage break up was certainly one of the hardest. I don't have any desire to relive it. I can't promise you that no one will show up at your door looking for me. Just like Sam, and Dalton can't promise the same. But I need a place to stay until my flight home at the end of the week, and I can't afford to book another place." He slid his hands into his pockets. "Are you really going to leave me with no place to go just because someone is looking for me?"

"No, of course not." Mary glanced over at Suzie, then looked back at Charlie. "We just need to ensure that everyone in Dune House remains safe."

"Oh, do you?" Charlie grinned at Mary and slid his hands back out of his pockets. "Does that include me? Are you going to keep me safe?"

"Charlie, we expect you to do your best to keep whatever drama you're in the middle of, out of this house." Suzie locked her eyes to his.

"I'll do what I can." Charlie shrugged, then continued past them into the kitchen. "Right now, I'm starving. Do you mind if I scavenge a bit?"

"There are some leftovers in the fridge, and stuff to make sandwiches." Mary frowned. "Help yourself."

Suzie leaned close to her and whispered in her ear, "You would keep anyone fed, wouldn't you?"

"Yes." Mary sighed. "But I'm going to be watching him like a hawk." She followed Charlie into the kitchen.

CHAPTER 11

Suzie remained close to Mary until Charlie headed back out onto the beach. Once they were alone in the dining room again, she called Mary over to the table.

"What did you think of his behavior?"

"I think he knows that we're onto something and he doesn't like it." Mary sat down beside Suzie. "I think he knows where that bag is, and he is just waiting for the opportunity to get out of here with it."

"Where do you think he would hide it?" Suzie shook her head. "Charlie was the only one who didn't go on the hike at the beach, which means that he had an opportunity to hide the gold somewhere."

"But where?" Mary skimmed through the

papers in front of her. "As far as I could see Charlie doesn't own any property here. He must have chosen a place he considered safe to stash it."

"That's if he took it at all." Suzie frowned. "We're assuming that it was one of the guests that took the bag, but what if there was someone else there?"

"Someone else?" Mary tipped her head to the side. "Like who?"

"Like Donald, or his son. Maybe they knew there was still a bag of gold in the mine. Maybe they took the opportunity to go back and look for it." Suzie sighed. "I know it doesn't make much sense that they would be able to sneak in between the time we found Jimmy, and the time that Jason and I returned. I mean they have had years to go down there. But what if someone did? Yes, Charlie has some things stacked up against him, but you and I both know that doesn't necessarily make him guilty."

"That's a good point. And add to that the fact that Scott might have known the gold was there, too. He would know about the layout of the mine. But again, how would he have known to go look for the gold on the same day we explored the mine? None of it was planned." Mary closed her eyes as she sat back in her chair. "It's too much of a coincidence."

"Unless, it was planned." Suzie cleared her throat. "Both Charlie and Sam were quite intent on getting into that corridor. It all looked coincidental to us, but it might have been orchestrated in some way."

"True. Maybe Scott planned to get to the gold, with Sam, or Charlie?" Mary nodded. "That's possible."

"It's time I paid another visit to Scott." Suzie stood up from the table. "I would like to know what really happened back then between him and Jimmy. He says it turned out to be a good thing for him that he was fired. But that doesn't mean he felt that way at the time. It's amazing how people can look at things with a positive state of mind when the crisis has passed."

"You're right about that." Mary stood up from the table. "I'm going to speak to Pam at the diner. She might remember something about Jimmy. She's been working at the diner for a very long time."

"I hadn't even thought about that, Mary. That is a great idea." Suzie grabbed her purse. "Let me know what you find out."

"You do the same." Mary caught up with her at

the door. "And Suzie, be careful. I feel like we're getting close to an answer here, and the closer we get the more dangerous things become."

"Now, who's being overprotective?" Suzie winked at her, then nodded. "I'll be careful, I promise."

It wasn't hard for Suzie to find Scott's current job. He had posted about it online, and she had been following him on social media ever since he became a potential suspect. She also knew that he usually used his lunch break to go to the gym. Instead of going into the factory where he worked, she parked outside of it, and waited for him to come out to make his journey to the gym. He would be in a more talkative mood away from work, she guessed.

Right on time, Scott stepped out of the factory and walked to his car. As she followed him through the streets of Parish, she wondered what it was like for him to be part of the crew that found the gold. All of those workers had been there that day. They had watched the mine's owners, and their relatives celebrate, knowing that their own lives wouldn't change. How difficult did it have to be for a man who had little, to carve gold from a mine and hand it over to a man who already had plenty?

Lost in thought, Suzie turned into the parking

lot behind Scott's car. It wasn't until she parked several spaces away from him that she looked up at the name of the gym. Her breath caught in her throat. Scott's gym was Lane Street Gym? The same name that was on the duffel bag that contained the gold?

Suzie's mind spun as she tried to make sense of this new development. Clearly, years had gone by since that bag had been left in the mine. But could it really be a coincidence that the duffel bag was from the same gym? She didn't have much time to think about it, as Scott walked quickly towards the gym door. She followed quickly after him, and caught up with him just inside the doors. He pulled his card out to show the receptionist but paused when Suzie interrupted him.

"Scott?"

"Yes?" He turned to face her, then frowned. "Ah, you again."

"Yes me." Suzie swallowed thickly as she continued to try to piece together how the gym connected to Jimmy Tomson. "I just wanted a few minutes of your time. If that's okay?"

"You'll have to run for it." Scott smiled as he studied her.

"Excuse me?" Suzie's heart skipped a beat.

"She's my guest, Kylie." Scott smiled at the receptionist.

"Go on in." Kylie smiled in return.

Suzie followed him into the gym, though she wasn't exactly dressed for it. He stepped onto a treadmill, then pointed to the one beside him.

"I only get an hour lunch, and I need to get my cardio in, so if you want to talk, then you have to run."

Suzie balked at the thought. She didn't mind a little exercise, but she couldn't remember the last time she was on a treadmill. If it made him willing to share, it would be worth it.

"Fine, I'll see if I can keep up." Suzie climbed onto the treadmill. "Have you been coming to this gym for a long time?"

"Close to forty years." As the machine whirred to life, he started to jog.

"So, you were coming here while you were working at the mine?" Suzie increased the speed a bit to keep up with him.

"Yes. The guys and I would come out here after a shift, or sometimes before. It was a good stress reliever." Scott stretched his arms above his head, then out beside him, as he continued to quicken his pace.

Suzie noticed for the first time his excellent physique. After years of hard labor, and years of going to the gym, she guessed that he was as strong as he looked.

"Did Jimmy come here with you?" Suzie braced herself as she touched on the sensitive subject.

"On about Jimmy again?" Scott glanced over at her. "No, he didn't come here. He didn't believe in spending money to do what he said he could do for free. But most of the workers came here because we got a discount. The co-owner of the mine, Donald, owns this gym too, or at least he did at the time, so he gave us a discount if we became members. Most of us did it, just to have a place to swim, and they have a sauna." He shrugged. "Can't beat that."

"That was nice of him. What about Terrance? Did he ever offer you a discount on something?" Suzie did her best to catch her breath as she jogged on the treadmill.

"Oh, I never even met Terrance. He was always working away. Apparently, he came to Garber around the time when the mine closed to thank the workers. But of course I never met him because I wasn't working there anymore." Scott increased his speed and broke into a full run. "No, that place pulled in a ton of cash. With the amount of gold we dug out, they would have been rolling in it. But it all dried up after a few years. That's why they closed the mine."

"Okay, I'm done." Suzie gasped for air as she turned the treadmill off. "I'm too old for this."

"Nonsense." Scott chuckled as he slowed down as well. "You're younger than me. You did pretty good, actually."

"Scott, be straight with me." Suzie leaned on the handle of the treadmill and looked at him. "Who wanted to see Jimmy dead?"

"Take your pick." Scott shrugged and used a towel to wipe off the back of his neck. "Jimmy liked to make enemies. I told you where to start. I really have nothing else to say about it. Now, I'm going to go enjoy my sauna." He stepped off the treadmill and walked away.

Suzie limped her way to the door. She wasn't sure that the information she got was worth the effort.

CHAPTER 12

Mary pushed open the door to the diner and stepped inside. With the lunch hour in full swing, the place was packed with people. She noticed Pam had her hands full with a large table. As Mary settled at an empty table, she couldn't help but wonder where Charlie might be. What was he up to right at that moment?

"Mary, let me grab you some tea." Pam whizzed by her with a flash of a smile.

"Thanks Pam." Mary smiled in return. She admired how spry and determined Pam was, though she had to be at least twenty years older than Mary. At the moment, Mary couldn't imagine being able to wait tables.

"Here you go." Pam placed a glass of iced tea on

the table in front of Mary, then she sat down in the chair across from her. "So dish."

"Dish?" Mary gazed at her. "Aren't you busy?"

"Not at the moment. All of my tables are taken care of, and everyone is talking about Jimmy Tomson." Pam raised an eyebrow.

"Actually, that's what I'm here to talk to you about." Mary took a sip of her tea. "Did you know him?"

"Yes, I did. Well, I didn't know him well, but I waited on him, often. Him, and Donald, the owner of the mine." Pam tipped her head towards the table in the back of the diner. "He and Donald would come in every Saturday morning and sit at that table."

"That's quite a ritual." Mary smiled at the thought. "They must have been good friends."

"Sometimes they were friends. Sometimes they would get into shouting matches and I'd have to kick them both out." Pam rolled her eyes. "Back then, men didn't take kindly to women pushing them around. But I still did it."

"I bet you did." Mary grinned. "I guess they stopped meeting after the mine closed."

"No, actually. They kept meeting here for a little while. I remember because I was surprised to see them both after the news about the mine closing spread. But those last few meetings, they weren't friendly ones." Pam pursed her lips.

"Did you have to kick them out for arguing?" Mary studied Pam's expression.

"No. It was different." Pam shuddered, then shook her head. "I had another waitress take over for me, because there was just this vibe I couldn't tolerate. It was like they hated each other, or worse." She looked across the table at Mary. "It's hard to explain."

"I think you've done pretty well." Mary smiled. "Did you ever see the other owner of the mine, Terrance?"

"Once." Pam nodded. "He came in here with Donald shortly after the mine closed. It was on Saturday, so I expected Jimmy to join them, but he never did."

"Maybe he was already dead." Mary opened her mouth to ask another question, but Pam hopped up from the table to take care of another customer.

Mary typed out a quick text to Suzie to update her on what she had learned. When she looked up from her phone again, she found a woman standing beside her.

"I'm Sarah." She extended her hand as she looked into Mary's eyes.

"Sarah?" Mary stared back at her as she gave her hand a brief shake.

"Charlie's wife." Sarah cleared her throat. "Ex-wife. Jenny is my daughter." She glanced over at the woman who watched them from a table near the back of the diner. "I know some of your guests filed a complaint against her today. I thought it would be best if I introduced myself and maybe explained a little bit of what's going on here."

"Thank you for that." Mary studied the woman's expression. "Some of our guests have said that Jenny was looking for Charlie and wouldn't leave them alone. She gave them quite a fright."

"Yes, we're both looking for Charlie." Sarah sighed, then clutched her hands together. "I just want some answers, and so does Jenny. When I heard that Jimmy Tomson was found in the mine, I just—" She frowned. "I always thought he took off. I never dreamed that Charlie could have done something to him."

"You think that Charlie is responsible for Jimmy's death?" Mary glanced over her shoulder to be sure that no one was close enough to hear, then turned back to Sarah and lowered her voice. "Do you have any reason to believe that?"

"Yes." Sarah frowned. "Jimmy and I were in love. Neither of us planned it. We broke up in high school and thought we were done with each other. I met Charlie and I thought he was the one. But over the years we drifted apart. Then I came into contact with Jimmy again, just by happenstance. Things picked up right where they left off, only far more intense." She blushed as she looked down at her hands. "It was wrong, I know it was. I planned to call it off with Jimmy. Then I found out I was pregnant." She looked up at Mary. "That changed everything."

"Jenny isn't Charlie's?" Mary's eyes widened, though she did her best to hide her shock. Her own unhappy marriage had some very strained points at times, but she couldn't imagine how her ex-husband would have reacted if he found out that one of their children wasn't his.

"I wasn't sure at first. I tried to convince myself that the baby couldn't be Jimmy's. But when I did the math it seemed pretty certain that she was. I sent Jimmy a letter to tell him. I didn't want to risk seeing him in person, I wasn't sure how he would react."

Sarah winced. "I know this is a lot to be telling you. But I feel like I need to tell someone. I don't know anyone here, and Charlie refuses to speak to me. I think he must have read the letter, or found out some other way, because he took off right after I sent it. He had a son from a previous relationship and took him with. I assumed that Jimmy got the letter, and took off, too, because he didn't want to be a parent. So, I was left raising Jenny on my own." She took a step closer to Mary and lowered her voice. "When I heard that it was Jimmy Tomson they found, I became suspicious that Charlie had killed him. I broke the news to Jenny, and she wanted to find out the truth. So, that's why we're here." She spread her hands out in front of her. "I can't know for sure what happened to Jimmy, but I do know that Charlie was the jealous sort. If I thought back then that there was any chance Charlie was involved in his disappearance, I would have said something."

"Now, you need to say something." Mary caught her hand and held it. "You need to go to the police with this information. It's important that they know that Charlie had this kind of motivation to kill Jimmy."

"But I don't know for sure that he did it." Sarah pulled her hand away and shivered. "What if I'm wrong? I already ruined Charlie's life once. I'm not sure that I can do it again. I just want to see him. I want to look him in the eye and ask him. I'm sure I'll be able to tell if he's lying."

"That may be what you want, Sarah, but you might want to consider what's best. Charlie could be a very dangerous man. Is it fair to let him run loose?" Mary took a sharp breath as Pam dropped a plate of food in front of her, then whisked off again. "I didn't order this."

"Eat, Mary." Pam waved her hand at her as she continued on to another table.

"I'll think about it." Sarah frowned. "But I wanted to assure you that you have nothing to worry about from us."

As Sarah walked away, Mary was not reassured. In fact, she was more concerned than ever. She was also very, very hungry. As she dug into her food, she noticed Sarah and Jenny leave the diner. She ate slowly, hoping that Pam would have more time to talk. But more and more customers filled the diner. Finally, she left the cash for her food and a tip, and left the diner. She hadn't heard back from Suzie yet, and was curious about what she thought about Donald and Jimmy's meetings. When she parked in front of Dune House, she noticed Jason's car parked there as well. Intrigued, she hurried up to the front porch, where she met Suzie just outside the door.

"Mary, it would be best if we stayed outside." Suzie put her hand on Mary's arm and guided her back away from the front door.

"Why? What's happening inside?" Mary shifted away from Suzie's touch and peered through the front door.

"Jason felt he had enough information to arrest Charlie." Suzie looked through the door as well. "I'm not sure if I agree with him, but he has to do his job. I guess he was getting some pressure from the higher-ups about not getting his case solved. Anyway, he says he's just going to keep him for a forty-eight hour hold, unless he can get Charlie to confess to something. He's hoping the time behind bars will rattle Charlie a bit and shake free some details about the crime."

"He's in there now? With Charlie? I just spoke with his ex-wife not that long ago. I encouraged her to go to the police with the information she had. Maybe she did." Mary raised an eyebrow then stepped back as the front door swung open and Jason escorted Charlie through it.

Charlie briefly met Suzie's eyes, then Mary's

before Jason guided him down the front steps of the porch.

"I don't feel real safe right now," Charlie muttered.

"I'm going to send a few officers over to do a search of the room." Jason paused long enough to nod to Suzie and Mary. "I'll be in touch."

"You have no right to do any of this." Charlie jerked forward.

"We'll discuss it at the station." Jason's grasp remained strong as he propelled Charlie towards the parking lot, and his waiting car.

Suzie stepped closer to Mary as she clutched at the collar of her blouse. "What if we're wrong, Mary? What if Charlie had nothing to do with any of this?"

"He had a very good reason to do it." Mary pursed her lips as she watched Jason's car pull out of the parking lot. "Jason wouldn't have arrested him without good reason."

"You're right." Suzie let her hands fall back to her sides. "But honestly, something still doesn't feel right. I need more information about the mine, and what was really going on behind closed doors."

"Maybe Louis can help?" Mary glanced at her.

"I should talk to the others and let them know what's happening."

"Are you sure you want to do that on your own?" Suzie touched her arm.

"Yes, I'll be fine, Suzie. Go find out what you can. We need to find out what's going on here before things get any more out of control." Mary took her hand and gave it a light squeeze. "I can handle this."

"I know you can. Thanks, Mary." Suzie headed down the steps. She decided to walk to the library, it wasn't far, and she needed the fresh air. Her thoughts were a jumble as she tried to pinpoint whether she agreed with Charlie's arrest or not. She could understand why Jason made the decision, but she wasn't sure that he was on the right track. After finding out that Donald lied about seeing Jimmy after the mine closed, she was torn about who might have more to hide.

CHAPTER 13

S uzie stepped into the library and found Louis at his desk.

"Hi Louis." She sat down beside him. "I wanted to check in and see if you had found any more information for me about Jimmy?"

"I do have some information. But I'll only tell you if you're willing to tell me about what just happened at Dune House." Louis flashed her a smile.

"What do you mean?" Suzie's eyes widened. "How did you hear already?"

"What's going on in Garber." Louis pointed to his computer screen. "Everyone posts on here. Someone saw Jason at Dune House and saw him leave with someone in the back seat."

CINDY BELL

"Wow." Suzie leaned back in her chair. "I had no idea that site even existed."

"Yes, well now you know." Louis looked at her expectantly.

"So, what do you have to share?" Suzie asked.

"I spoke to my father." Louis smiled sadly. "His memory isn't the best, but he remembered a few things from when the mine closed."

"He did?" Suzie sat up straighter.

"Apparently, Terrance lived in Parish before he went to France. That's how Donald met him. My dad knew Terrance, although he was quite a few years older than Terrance." Louis sat forward slightly. "Terrance came to town shortly after the mine closed. He wanted to speak to the workers and tie up some business affairs."

"Scott, an employee of the mine, just told me that as well." Suzie smiled.

"Well, my dad owned the local convenience store in those days. Terrance came in to buy a few bits and pieces," Louis explained. "Terrance asked my dad if he had seen Jimmy recently. When Dad said he hadn't, Terrance mentioned if he did could he tell Jimmy to call him. Apparently, Jimmy had asked to meet with Terrance in private about something. Jimmy had never turned up to the

154

meeting, he just disappeared. Obviously, Terrance wanted to meet with Jimmy to find out what he had to say."

"Interesting." Suzie nodded. "Do you have any idea what it was about?"

"No, like I said it probably means nothing." Louis smiled. "But I just wanted to let you know."

"It might be something, though." Suzie nodded.

"You might want to tell Jason. Just in case."

"I will do that." Suzie stood up. "Thank you, Louis."

"Wait!" Louis stood up quickly. "You promised?"

"Right, sorry." Suzie hesitated, then nodded. "It was Charlie. But please, keep that to yourself. At this point I'm not sure who to suspect."

"I won't say a word." Louis sank down into his chair again.

When Suzie returned to Dune House, she found Mary alone in the dining room with the remnants of a snack spread out on the table.

"How did it go?" Suzie sat down beside her.

"I think everyone was a little relieved. Sam acted odd, as expected. He didn't say a word, and then just got up and left. All of them did. Dalton suggested they visit the maritime museum to get their minds off everything." Mary began to gather the plates scattered around the table.

"Leave it, Mary. I found out something from Louis." Suzie explained what Louis had said. "Maybe it was about the thefts."

"Interesting." Mary nodded. "Maybe Jimmy stole the gold?"

"But if Jimmy wanted to speak to Terrance about the stealing, he wouldn't be the one doing it, would he?"

"That's true. Unless he wanted to put the blame on someone else to cover his tracks." Mary picked the plates up and walked towards the sink.

"Scott said that Jimmy never went to the gym, so I wonder who that gym bag belonged to. It is still possible it was Jimmy's, but maybe it wasn't."

"You're right." Mary placed the plates in the sink.

"I wonder if there was any animosity between Terrance and Donald." Suzie sat forward. "Donald was stuck in a partnership with Terrance. He did all the work, ran the mine, but according to Louis, Terrance still claimed half of the profit because of his original investments."

"Maybe." Mary shrugged. "If there was no more

gold there and the mine was closing, maybe that put more pressure on both of them."

"That's possible." Suzie sighed as she sat back in her chair. "We know that Charlie had plenty of motive to go after Jimmy. We also know that according to just about everyone there was no love lost between Scott and Jimmy. Scott's the one that tipped us off to the idea that someone was stealing from the mine. Maybe that was just a way for him to deter suspicion from himself."

"But Charlie came back here." Mary winced and shook her head. "That's the part that makes me think he had something to do with this. He came back here and found Jimmy. He led us right to the mine. Why would he do that if he didn't know that Jimmy was there?"

"Why would he do it, if he knew that Jimmy was there?" Suzie raised her eyebrows. "That's the reason I think maybe it's too easy to assume he was involved. If he is really the person who killed Jimmy, why would he return just to implicate himself?"

"Because he knew about the gold?" Mary shrugged. "Maybe that was enough reason for him to want Jimmy found, just so he could get to the gold."

"But he didn't need us around to get to it." Suzie rubbed a hand along her forehead. "He could have just gone in himself."

"Unless he needed a partner for some reason. We know that he and Sam were discussing how to speak to the police. Which makes me think that they were working together to hide something." Mary stood up from the table. "Maybe it's time we find out what Sam was up to, and learn a little bit more about him. Dalton seems like someone who would be willing to have a reasonable conversation. Tiffany said that they've been friends since college. Maybe he knows something about Sam that can help us figure out what he was doing with Charlie."

"That's a good idea, Mary. But I think you should talk to him by yourself. You have a kinder way with people, and I'm sure that Dalton will be more comfortable if one person is asking him questions instead of two." Suzie gathered up the papers on the table. "I want to see if I can talk to Donald about what Jimmy might have wanted to speak to Terrance about. I doubt I'll be able to speak to him, though. So, I'll try to speak to Bob and see what he knows about his father's business with the mine, and Jimmy Tomson."

"Do you think he'll talk to you?" Mary paused in the doorway of the kitchen and looked back at her.

"I don't think I'm going to give him a choice." Suzie smiled, then headed out through the front door.

CHAPTER 14

$\mathcal{M}$ary stepped out onto the porch, with Pilot at her side. Pilot began to bark as he looked down the beach. Mary spotted Dawn and Dalton. She guessed they had finished with the museum and decided to spend some time on the beach. She watched as Dalton splashed through the waves that washed up on the sand. She guessed that his feet had to be freezing as the water wasn't warm enough for swimming. But he didn't seem to mind. Dawn lingered just beyond the water. She seemed to be amused by Dalton's antics, but every time the water came anywhere near her, she jumped back and squealed. Mary could see the connection between them, and yet they both appeared to hold back. She hadn't seen them kiss, or hug. She hadn't noticed any hint of secret meetups. And yet there it was, plain for anyone to see, the electricity between them.

As Dalton and Dawn began to walk back towards the house, Pilot raced out across the sand to greet them. It would be tough to get to talk to Dalton alone, since Dawn stuck by his side at all times.

"Hi, you two." Mary smiled as they reached the stairs that led up to the porch. "Did you have fun out there?"

"That water is cold." Dalton grinned and brushed some sand from his feet. "I wish I could go for a swim, it looks so beautiful, but I just can't bring myself to dive in."

"You're crazy." Dawn laughed. "I couldn't even imagine going for a swim in that icy water. But it does make me want to come back for a visit when it's warmer."

"We'd be happy to have you." Mary smiled at her. "The water is so lovely in the summer, just cool enough to be refreshing on a hot day."

"Ah yes, a good swim would certainly put my mind at ease right now." Dalton closed his eyes briefly, then ran his hand back through his hair. "Each time I start to relax, I think about Charlie in that jail cell, and whether I could have done anything to stop all of this from happening."

"You couldn't travel back through time and stop Charlie from killing Jimmy." Dawn shook her head. "There's nothing that you could have done."

"That is if Charlie did it, Dawn." Dalton met her eyes. "We don't know that for sure."

"Even if he didn't, us coming here is the reason all of this came to light." Dawn sighed. "Maybe some things are better left undiscovered."

"Not this." Mary stepped aside so that they could get past her on the porch. "A person's life should never just disappear."

"No, it shouldn't disappear, but maybe it's better left alone." Dawn shrugged. "I'm just saying, who is it going to benefit to find out what really happened to Jimmy?"

"Him." Dalton looked up at both of them. "It will benefit him. He didn't ask to be murdered or left in that mine. He didn't ask for his life to be cut short."

"You're right." Mary nodded as she studied Dalton's stricken expression. "Jimmy deserves some closure. Dalton, would you mind if we talked for a moment?"

"Sure." Dalton leaned back against the railing and met her eyes.

Dawn lingered by his side, close to him.

Mary considered a few different options to politely extricate her from the conversation but decided against it. Sending Dawn away could set a tense tone, and she didn't want to do that.

"I know you and Sam have been friends for some time, right?" Mary smiled at Dalton.

"Yes." Dalton's jaw tensed.

"I can see the two of you behave a bit like brothers." Mary watched as Dalton's eyes narrowed just enough for her to notice.

"Yes, you could say that." Dalton looked over at Dawn. "Give us a minute, will you?"

"Oh, I don't mind staying." Dawn gazed at him with a tight smile on her lips.

"Dawn." Dalton tipped his head towards the dining room door. "Go on, I'll be right in."

"Okay." Dawn glanced at Mary, then stepped through the door into the dining room.

Dalton shifted into a standing position and crossed his arms as he looked at Mary. "Why are you asking me about Sam?"

"I'm just curious about him. He doesn't say much. It's hard to get a read on him. I thought you might be able to give me an idea of how I can make him feel more comfortable." Mary noted the sudden sternness in his tone, and the change in his posture. Did he intend to intimidate her, or was it a subconscious attempt?

"You don't need to worry about Sam. He does his own thing. That's just who he is." Dalton scratched his fingertips through his hair then shrugged. "Things like this, they don't bother him the way they do other people."

"No?" Mary tipped her head to the side. "I guess he's a little detached from it all?"

"He just doesn't get caught up in the small things. You don't need to worry about making him comfortable." Dalton started to step past her.

"I just noticed that he and Charlie seemed pretty close, and with Charlie in custody, I thought he might be a little upset." Mary matched his movements, so that they remained the same distance apart.

"He doesn't know Charlie any better than the rest of us." Dalton locked his eyes to hers. "Sam has nothing to do with any of this. Got it?"

Mary raised an eyebrow as Dalton stared straight at her. She felt her heartbeat quicken. In all the time he'd been at Dune House she'd never once felt uncomfortable around him. But in that moment, she wished that she wasn't alone with him. Pilot gave a soft bark, as if to remind her that she wasn't alone.

"I understand." Mary forced a smile to her lips. "Let me know if you or Dawn need anything."

"Sure." Dalton turned and stepped into the house.

Mary crouched down and began to stroke Pilot's fur.

"What do you think, buddy? Exactly what kind of mess are we in the middle of here?"

As Mary straightened up again, she caught sight of Sam as he ran along the beach. He didn't run like many other runners she saw on the beach. His strides weren't paced, his breathing wasn't regular. He ran as if he had something to run from, and perhaps, some rage to set free. As he drew closer, she wondered if she should head inside before he could reach her. It was clear to her that Dalton was hiding something about Sam. Did he know about Sam's involvement with Charlie? Did he know about the gold? If Dalton and Sam were as close as they seemed to be, then she guessed Sam would tell Dalton all about it. Now that she'd seen a more intense side of Dalton, she could believe that he might be involved. Why else would he have sent Dawn away when she started asking about Sam? Was he hiding something?

Just as Sam reached the edge of the property, Mary stepped into the dining room, with Pilot at her side. When she glanced back through the thick glass, she caught sight of Sam's eyes settled on her. Did he see her? Did he mean for her to see him, watching her?

Pilot gave her hand a hard nudge as he whined.

Mary blinked, then turned away from the door. She led Pilot into the kitchen to get him a treat. When she heard the dining room door open, her muscles tensed. When she heard it snap shut, she held her breath. Heavy footsteps echoed on the stairs that led up from the kitchen. She heard a door open and close. Only then did she breathe again. Sam seemed to have gone out of his way not to say a word to her. Had he noticed that she did the same?

CHAPTER 15

Suzie entered the warehouse without anyone noticing. In fact, she realized there were very few people working in a very large building. She wondered if the company had recently been through some layoffs. Not far in, she saw Bob strolling through rows of shelving.

"Bob." Suzie called out to him before he could get too far from her.

"Suzie?" Bob turned to look at her. "What are you doing here? I have nothing to say to you." He turned and started to walk away.

"Bob, I want to speak to your father." Suzie walked towards him.

"He isn't seeing anyone." Bob quickened his pace.

"In that case I would like to speak with you for a second, would you mind?" Suzie followed him through the warehouse.

"I really can't, I have a busy schedule today." Bob glanced up from his clipboard long enough to shoot a harsh look in her direction. "Besides, I've had enough of your games. As far as I'm concerned you and my father made a deal, it has nothing to do with me."

"That's not true. It has a lot to do with you." Suzie quickened her pace to keep up with him as he continued through the warehouse. "In fact, I think that everything that is happening right now has a lot to do with you. You remember Jimmy, don't you?" She pulled up a picture on her phone and held it up in the air. "This is you, isn't it? With the gold nugget?"

Bob froze, then lowered his clipboard. As he turned to look at the phone, his cheeks reddened.

"That was a long time ago."

"You must have thought you would be rich." Suzie smiled as she glanced at his wide-eyed expression in the photograph, then looked back at him. "To a boy as young as you were, finding gold must have seemed like a dream come true."

"Of course, it did. It was." Bob studied the

picture. "Things were so different then. Everyone was so happy."

"You mean, your dad was?" Suzie took a step closer to him. "He looks pretty happy."

"My dad, yes. Which made everyone else in our household happy." Bob looked away from the phone and met her eyes. "It should have kept us all happy for life."

"But it didn't, did it?" Suzie looked around the warehouse. "I noticed that this place is up for auction."

"That's not your business. Unless you're interested in buying it." Bob pressed the clipboard against his chest. "Gold doesn't last forever."

"No, but it sure seemed to vanish a lot faster than it should have, didn't it?" Suzie cleared her throat as she held out the paperwork in her hand. "I heard that there were quite a few accusations going around about gold being stolen."

"None of that has anything to do with me." Bob scowled and started to turn away. "I was just a kid."

"I'm just trying to find out the truth for Jimmy. He was in that mine for decades, Bob. Don't you think it's time that people stopped keeping secrets about it?" Suzie searched his eyes. "What got him killed?"

"I don't know. I was just a kid." Bob turned away from her. "If I see you on my property again, I will call the police and press charges for trespassing." He hurried towards the other side of the warehouse.

Suzie bit into her bottom lip. She wondered if she had pushed things too far. She sensed something in Bob, fear, or maybe guilt. Her instincts told her to press him. But perhaps that was the wrong choice. It seemed to her that any secrets Bob might have, he intended to keep for as long as he could. She wasn't one to let things go, however.

Bob had gone from a little boy who had likely been given everything thanks to his father's riches, to a businessman who faced the loss of everything he owned. That kind of stress and pressure would wear on him. She intended to be right there when he was ready to crack. At the moment though, she had other things to focus on.

As Suzie returned to her car, her cell phone rang. She pulled it from her pocket and smiled at the sight of Paul's name.

"Hi Paul."

"Suzie. What have you been doing?"

"What's wrong?" Suzie noticed the tension in his voice.

"I just got a call from Donald. He said that if you speak to his son again, he'll involve the authorities, or other resources, to keep you out of his business." Paul took a sharp breath. "I thought I told you to stay away from them."

"I literally just left Bob." Suzie looked back towards the warehouse. "I must have really rattled him if he called his father that fast."

"Don't sound proud, Suzie." Paul sighed. "The point is, you're putting yourself in danger."

"Listen Paul, I can handle a few disgruntled businessmen. This is good news. This means I touched a nerve." Suzie settled into her car and started the engine.

"That's what I'm worried about. I'll be there for dinner tonight." The line cut off.

Suzie sent a quick text to Mary letting her know there would be one more for dinner.

Suzie took a deep breath as she backed out of the parking spot. She understood Paul's concern. But she couldn't deny a subtle thrill that rushed through her. She'd pushed a button, which meant that Bob could be close to revealing something. She didn't know how yet, but in her opinion, Bob knew something about Jimmy's death.

Mary watched the knife slice through the carrot as she prepared vegetables to add to the soup she'd put together for dinner. She wanted to create a setting of extreme comfort, enhanced by homemade bread rolls, warm soup, and a great opportunity for everyone to talk. But her thoughts kept shifting back to Sam. He was too young to be responsible for Jimmy's death, that much she knew. But if he was as detached as Dalton claimed, he probably wouldn't have had any trouble taking the gold from a skeleton. But Charlie had to be the one to tell him that the gold was there. Didn't he? She sighed as she looked up from the vegetables. It was hard to pinpoint the source of the unrest that rumbled through her, but she knew it had to do with missing something. There was some piece of the puzzle that she just couldn't get to fit together.

"Hey, sweetheart." Wes leaned against the doorway of the kitchen and gazed at her. "You doing okay?"

"I thought I told you to enjoy the sunset on the porch." Mary smiled as she looked over at him.

"You can't expect me to enjoy something like that without you by my side." Wes stepped farther into the kitchen. "You look so tense, Mary. All of this is weighing too heavily on your shoulders." He ran his hands along the curve of her shoulders and gave her a soft massage.

"You're distracting me." Mary huffed as she rushed over to the stove to turn down the temperature. "I have to get these vegetables into the pan before it gets too hot."

"Let me help you." Wes picked up the knife from the cutting board. "I'll finish the carrots."

"You don't have to do that." Mary turned back to take the knife from him.

"Mary." Wes gazed at her until she met his eyes. "Let me help you."

Mary released a slow breath to calm her nerves. She didn't want to argue. She didn't want to point out that she wasn't accustomed to relying on anyone's help anymore, and in fact, maybe a part of her was afraid of it, after the outcome of her marriage. But instead she focused her attention on adding the vegetables to the pot.

"Hurry please, everything needs to go in."

"Here you go." Wes carried the cutting board with the sliced carrots on it over to her. "It smells delicious."

"I'm glad you think so." Mary used the knife to

push the carrots into the pan. As they splashed into the boiling broth, she clenched her teeth. The last thing she wanted was for Wes to feel as if she didn't appreciate his kindness. "Thank you, Wes." She turned to face him, and found his arms spread out to draw her into a hug. She smiled as he wrapped them around her. He didn't say a word. He just held her against him. The rumbling within her began to settle. The pure comfort of his embrace was enough to make every muscle in her body relax.

"Wow! What is that delicious smell?" Tiffany stepped into the kitchen, then gasped. "Oh, I'm sorry. I didn't mean to interrupt."

"It's all right." Wes smiled as he pulled away. "We were just enjoying the delicious aroma ourselves."

"It'll be ready in just a few minutes." Mary's cheeks flushed as she hid her face from Tiffany.

"Great. I'm starving. Anything I can do to help?" Tiffany looked between the two of them.

"If you'd like to put some bowls out onto the table that would be great." Mary smiled as she pulled a stack of bowls down from the cabinet and handed them over to Tiffany.

Once Tiffany stepped into the dining room, Wes looked at Mary. "So, she's allowed to help?"

"It's complicated." Mary flashed him a smile, then stirred the soup.

"I'd love to talk about it sometime." Wes stepped up beside her.

"Maybe. But now, I'd rather focus on making this a wonderful dinner for everyone. Relaxed tongues share more secrets." Mary took a breath of the steam that rose from the soup, then picked up the pepper and sprinkled some more in.

"I'll keep that in mind." Wes smiled as he leaned close, then placed a light kiss on her cheek.

"I think Paul should be here by now. Maybe you should meet him on the porch?" Mary ducked away as he pulled back from the kiss. Her cheeks burned. Had Tiffany seen that? She wasn't sure why it mattered.

"All right, all right. I'll take the hint." Wes winked at her, then headed towards the front door.

Mary breathed a sigh of relief once she was alone in the kitchen. That sigh turned into a gasp, as another voice spoke up from a few steps behind her.

"You're torturing me."

Mary spun around and nearly bumped into Sam. He took the spoon from her hand and smiled as he leaned over the pot to give the contents a slow stir.

"I can't wait to have some of this."

"I'm glad." Mary stumbled over her words as she took the spoon back.

"Mary." Sam remained close to her as he spoke. "Is everything okay? I know this is a lot of stress on both you and Suzie. I feel like you're constantly worried about us, but no one is checking in on you."

"I'm checked on, trust me." Mary grinned, then blushed, then looked back at the soup. Her skin crawled as he continued to linger. "It's kind of you to ask, though."

"I thought I should ask about you. Since, I hear that you've been asking about me." Sam coughed.

Mary dropped the spoon into the soup. Some of the hot water splashed onto her hand. She yelped and jumped back, which caused her to bump into Sam's shoulder.

"Easy now." Sam caught her by the arms to steady her. "You need to be more careful." His grasp tightened.

"Tiffany." Mary called out as she tried to ignore the burning of her skin. "Plates, we need plates, too."

"Sure." Tiffany stepped into the kitchen. She paused at the sight of Sam. "Oh Sam, I didn't even know you were in here. Do you want to grab some spoons?"

"Glad to help." Sam smiled as he released Mary. "You should get some cold water on that hand." He tipped his head towards the sink, then took the spoons from Tiffany.

Mary held her breath until he left the kitchen. Only then did she allow herself to shudder. It couldn't have just been her imagination that he had sent her a clear warning, could it?

"Mary, are you okay?" Tiffany stepped closer to her.

"Yes, just a little splash of hot water. I'm fine." Mary rinsed her hand beneath cold water, then turned back to the soup. Her hand trembled as she stirred it. She thought that Charlie being behind bars would make Dune House feel safe, instead she felt more uneasy than ever. She turned the soup down, then checked the rolls in the oven. They were brown enough to take out. As she pulled the pan out of the oven, she felt another shiver carry through her. Perhaps Suzie's suspicion was right. Perhaps the wrong person was behind bars.

CHAPTER 16

Suzie walked up the steps to Dune House, just as Wes stepped through the front door and onto the porch.

"Hi Wes." Suzie smiled at him.

"Hey Suzie." Wes rubbed his hands together, then glanced past her. "Where's Paul?"

"I'm not sure. He said he would be here." Suzie tipped her head towards the door. "Who's inside?"

"I only saw Tiffany so far. Not sure who else." Wes stretched his arms above his head. "But I can tell you that dinner smells delicious."

"Wonderful, I could use a pick-me-up." Suzie paused beside him. "Hey Wes, if you had a duffel bag full of gold, where would you hide it?"

"Playing detective, I see." Wes raised an eyebrow. "That shouldn't surprise me."

"Answer the question." Suzie grinned.

"I think I would keep it close." Wes shrugged. "It might seem wise to stash it somewhere that no one could find, but I'd worry about not being able to get to it quickly. Especially if I thought someone else might know about it. I'd find a good, safe place to hide it, somewhere that I could be close to it for most of the day, or at least overnight."

"Interesting." Suzie narrowed her eyes. She had assumed that the guests wouldn't risk hiding the bag in Dune House, but now she wondered if she might be mistaken. What if the duffel bag, which they presumed was full of gold, was under their roof the entire time?

"Soup is almost ready." Wes tipped his head towards the house. "But it's a little tense in there."

"I imagine so." Suzie took a deep breath, then opened the front door. Wes followed her inside.

"Everything is ready." Mary called out as she carried a bowl of bread rolls to the table.

"Mary, are you okay?" Suzie frowned as she spotted the raised and reddened skin on her hand.

"Fine, just a bit of a kitchen catastrophe." Mary

waved her hand and smiled. "Let's eat, I'm starving."

Soon everyone was assembled at the table. Suzie paid special attention to Sam as he served himself a large bowl of soup. While the others chatted around him, he didn't say a word. His focus was on the food, as if his only goal was to fill his stomach.

The front door swung open and Paul stepped inside.

"Evening everyone." He smiled as he hung his jacket up by the front door.

"Paul, I'm so glad that you could make it." Suzie stood up to greet him. "The soup is still hot."

"Great." Paul gave her a quick hug then sat down at the table.

For a few minutes Suzie forgot all about the skeleton in the mine, and the missing bag. She just enjoyed the sounds of a happy gathering, and the smells of a delicious meal.

As Suzie began to clear the dishes from the table, Mary joined her with her own pile of dishes.

"Wes said something interesting to me outside." Suzie set the dishes in the sink, then looked at Mary. "He said if he found gold, he would hide it somewhere close to him. Somewhere that he could keep an eye on it."

"I suppose that would make sense." Mary added her dishes to the sink. "What do you think?"

"I think he might be right. No one knows this area well enough to hide the gold somewhere, maybe not even Charlie, as things have changed since he was last here." Suzie shrugged.

"If you think that the gold could be here, then there is only one thing we can do. See if we can find out who might have it in their room." Mary glanced over her shoulder at the group of guests seated around the table. "I'm thinking that we should tell them that we are going to be checking their rooms to make sure that they have enough towels, other supplies and their beds are made. That way we can see their reactions. If anyone reacts or objects, then that is the most likely person to have stolen and hidden the gold. Then we can tell Jason our suspicions."

"Clever idea." Suzie nodded. "I think Sam or Dalton are the most likely people to have the gold. The police already searched Charlie's room and didn't find anything when he was arrested. If we don't get a reaction, we can check other places. I really want to know what happened to the bag, don't you?" She looked back at Mary.

"Yes, I do." Mary frowned. "But how can we

even tell them that we are going to make up their rooms when they're all in for the night? I doubt they will want us in their rooms while they are at Dune House, so we might take their reactions the wrong way."

"I have an idea." Suzie smiled, then walked back over to the table. She touched Paul on the shoulder, then gestured for him to join her in the kitchen. After collecting a few plates, she headed into the kitchen.

Paul picked up two empty glasses and followed after her.

"I know you're up to something." Paul smiled as he set the glasses in the sink. "I saw you over there whispering with Mary."

"I need a favor." Suzie turned around to face him and smiled.

"Another favor?" Paul took her hands in his. "What is it this time?"

"I want you to make a big deal about the ice cream parlor in town and then offer to take the guests to it. I know it might be a bit too cold for ice cream for some of them, but they also have delicious hot fudge sauce and delicious pies. Mary and I will stay back to clean up and check that everything is okay in the guests' rooms." Suzie shrugged as she grasped his hands. "Nothing too major, right? You like ice cream and pie."

"So, you want me to get everyone out of your hair for some reason. Do I want to know what that reason is?" Paul leaned closer to her as he smiled. "Or should I just be grateful to be ignorant?"

"Gratitude is always a good way to go." Suzie kissed his cheek. "Will you do it?"

"Of course, I will." Paul shrugged.

"And make sure Wes goes with you." Suzie glanced into the dining room.

"I bet he's going to be pretty curious about this." Paul caught her eye once more before he headed back into the dining room.

Suzie turned to the sink, then listened as Paul talked up the ice cream parlor. She knew it was out of his comfort zone to promote anything, or to be so candid with strangers, but he still did a good job of it. By the time he was finished, everyone had agreed to join him, including Wes.

"Mary, I'll grab your jacket." Wes stood up from the table as Suzie stepped back into the dining room.

"Oh no, there's no need." Mary raised her voice. "I'm going to stay behind and get things cleaned up. We want to check on the rooms while everyone's out, so we don't bother them. Maybe you could bring me something back?" Mary smiled as she looked at the guests' faces. None of them reacted. Dawn wasn't in the room, she was already on the porch. But she doubted that Dawn had the bag.

"Sure, I can." Wes gazed at her for a moment, then looked over at Suzie. His brow furrowed, but he followed after Paul without saying another word.

As soon as the others were out the door, Suzie and Mary abandoned the dishes in the sink and turned to each other.

"Well, that didn't work. Did it?" Mary frowned. "No one reacted when we said we were going to go into their rooms."

"I know. Dawn was outside, but I doubt she has the bag." Suzie sighed. "I guess we have to clean their rooms now. They are going to be gone for at least an hour. That will give us plenty of time to check and restock their rooms like we said we would and finish cleaning up the kitchen." She started up the steps in the kitchen. "You start with Dalton's room. I'll start will Sam's."

Mary pushed open the door to Dalton's room.

Suzie stepped into Sam's room. Right away she was struck by a strange odor. It took her a few seconds to realize that it was coming from his running shoes. She waved a hand in front of her nose then opened the closet to get an extra blanket to put on his bed. She went into the bathroom and saw that he had enough towels and supplies. She took one more look around, then stepped out of Sam's room. She pulled the door closed behind her and started towards Dalton's room to help Mary, when she heard the creak of a floorboard. Her heart jumped into her throat as she turned in the direction of the sound. Dawn stood at the end of the hallway.

"What were you doing in Sam's room?" Dawn frowned.

"I was just checking to see if he needed new towels, or other supplies." Suzie held her breath as Dawn walked towards her.

"Didn't you do that this morning?" Dawn crossed her arms.

"We did, but like we mentioned tonight, we were going to recheck the rooms. We wanted to make sure that everyone had extra blankets because the temperature is meant to drop tonight," Suzie explained. "I thought you would have gone out with the others." She smiled. "What are you doing back so soon? Didn't you want something sweet?"

"I forgot something I needed." Dawn blushed, then glanced away. "I was just going to head back to join them now. But honestly, I don't think it's right for you to be in our rooms without telling us."

"We did tell the guests, you were on the porch, but I'm sorry if it's left you uneasy." Suzie did her best to soften her voice. "It's just that we don't like to disturb the guests, so we check on the rooms when everyone is out, if possible."

"I still think it's a little weird." Dawn crossed her arms. "But then I guess they do similar things at hotels. Do you have a do not disturb sign that I can hang on my door?"

"Oh, you don't need a sign. If you'd rather we not go into your room just let us know, and we'll be sure to stay out of it." Suzie glanced over her shoulder towards the stairs. "Are you going to go back and join them? The ice cream and pies are delicious."

"Yes, I'm looking forward to trying it. By the way, where is Mary? I don't see why you both need to stay back to clean up. Why don't you come join us? We can all pitch in to clean up later." Dawn smiled. "Mary? Where are you?"

"Oh no, we'd rather just get it done so we can all relax in front of the fire later." Suzie shrugged, but her heart pounded. She knew that Mary was in Dalton's room, and she had no idea if Mary was aware that Dawn was outside in the hall. After seeing how Dawn reacted when she knew that she had been in Sam's room, she could only imagine how she would react when she saw Mary coming out of Dalton's room.

"That's silly. You should come along." Dawn grabbed her hand and gave it a tug. "Hurry, before the place closes."

"I found it, Suzie! I found the bag!" Mary burst out of Dalton's room into the hallway.

"Found what?" Dawn crossed her arms.

"Oh dear." Mary froze.

"Are you sure, Mary?" Suzie looked over at her.

"I'm positive." Mary swallowed hard. "It's hidden under the blankets in the closet in Dalton's room. I was getting him an extra blanket to put at the end of his bed. The blankets and towels were such a mess that I wanted to refold them. It was hidden there under the blankets."

"What is?" Dawn looked between them both. "What is going on here?"

"That's what we're going to find out." Suzie

pulled out her phone and dialed Jason's number. She wasn't sure how Dalton was involved, or whether Jason would be able to link him to Jimmy's killer, but she was certain that he would know what to do. As soon as he answered, she started telling her story. "Mary just found the missing bag. I think you should come down here."

"Slow down, Suzie. Are you sure about this?" Jason asked.

"Yes Jason. It's in one of the guest's rooms." Suzie caught sight of Dawn sending a text on her cell phone. "You'd better hurry, I think things are about to get very tense."

"I'll be right there." Jason ended the call as Dawn tucked her phone into her pocket.

"Did you just text Dalton?" Suzie looked at the young woman.

"I did." Dawn glared at her. "I thought he should know that you two were pawing through his things."

"That's not what we were doing." Suzie shook her head. "I think you would like to explain to Jason, when he gets here, why your boyfriend had the missing bag from the crime scene hidden in the closet in his room."

"Dalton and I are not seeing each other." Dawn

blushed, then shook her head. "I have no idea what you're talking about. As far as I'm concerned, the two of you could have hidden it in there. Maybe that's why you had Paul and Wes take us all out for ice cream, so that you would have time to plant evidence." She narrowed her eyes. "You may think that you can get away with this, but I'll tell you right now, I'll never let Dalton be framed. He is a good man, a very good man. He would never steal anything."

"If he's such a good man then why aren't you two together?" Suzie studied her. "It's easy to see the connection between the two of you. What is holding you back from taking it a step further?"

"I'm just not sure if I'm ready." Dawn huffed. "And that has nothing to do with what we're discussing right now."

"No, maybe it doesn't. Jason's here." Suzie gestured to the top of the stairs where Jason stood. She was glad that she had managed to get Dawn to stay by talking to her, until Jason got there.

"Good. I'm glad he's here. Maybe he can explain to you that you need to respect the privacy of your guests." Dawn turned to face Jason. "These two were rummaging through our things!"

CHAPTER 17

"*I*s that so?" Jason rested his hand on his belt and looked between the three women. "Does someone want to tell me what is going on here?"

"I can do better than tell you." Mary pointed to Dalton's still open door. "I can show you. I was getting Dalton an extra blanket and I found the missing bag. It was hidden under the blankets in Dalton's closet."

"Because the two of them put it there." Dawn scowled at Suzie and Mary. "They created this ruse to get us out of the house, and I happened to come back to get something I forgot, and what did I find?" She swung her hands through the air. "These two were going through our rooms! They had no right to be in there."

"Is that true, Suzie?" Jason shifted his weight from one foot to the other.

"We were in their rooms to check if they need cleaning and to replenish supplies. We wanted to make sure that there were enough blankets in their rooms. We tell everyone staying here that we would do that when they check in. Dawn wasn't in the room when we mentioned that we would check their rooms while they were out tonight." Suzie looked at Dawn. "It's all part of the agreement that you signed when you reserved the rooms."

"But that's not what you were doing. You were planting that bag of gold in Dalton's room, so that you could frame Dalton." Dawn pointed her finger straight at Mary. "Admit it. You just want someone to take the fall for the two of you. Of course, you're the ones who took the gold."

"Wait." Mary narrowed her eyes as she looked at Dawn. "How do you even know about the gold? No one else knows about it. The only way you could know is if you knew that someone took it in the first place."

"She has a point." Jason took a step closer to

Dawn. "Would you care to explain that?" He held up one hand as she shifted away from him. "Actually, let me take a look at this bag first. Mary?" He gestured to Dalton's room. "Would you like to show me?"

"Sure." Mary led the way into Dalton's room.

"You shouldn't be going in there!" Dawn took a step forward.

"Take it easy." Suzie moved between Dawn and Dalton's bedroom door.

After a few minutes, Jason stepped back out of the room. "Okay, it's there and it does have rocks with gold in it." He turned towards Dawn. "Now, would you like to explain to me how you knew about it, Dawn?"

"I want to hear about why they were in Dalton's room, first." Dawn crossed her arms. "Or maybe, Dalton would like to hear it for himself?" She stared at the top of the stairs, where Dalton stood.

"What exactly is going on here?" Dalton shoved past the others and glared at Jason.

"They said they found gold in your room, Dalton." Dawn looked at him.

"Gold? What gold?" Dalton's eyes widened. "Have you lost your mind?"

"Everyone, just calm down!" Jason held his hands out in front of him. "Dalton, I need to speak with you."

"No way." Dalton turned towards the stairs. "I'm not having any of this. I don't have to listen to a word you say."

"Dalton! Stop!" Jason's sharp voice whipped through the hallway.

"Take it easy. I'm not trying to cause any trouble here." Dalton turned back to face Jason. "I'm sorry, I got a little hot-headed. None of this makes any sense to me. I didn't have anything to do with any gold. I came here because Dawn sent me a text that said Mary was searching my room. I came back here, and I find you ready to arrest me. So yes, I was a little overwhelmed and I made a bad choice by walking away from you. But that's only because I haven't done anything wrong, and all of this scared me. So, if you need to arrest me for that, go ahead and get it over with."

"I'm not arresting anyone, yet." Jason kept his gaze on Dalton. "I think it would be best if we discussed this down at the station. If you're willing to comply, I can take you out the door with no cuffs on. But if you want to resist me, this is going to be a lot less pleasant."

"Fine." Dalton took a deep breath. "This is obviously a misunderstanding. It's best if we get it cleared up."

"Dalton, don't go with him." Dawn took a step towards him. "They're trying to frame you."

"Dawn, take it easy." Dalton met her eyes. "I'll get this all straightened out."

"Actually, I think it would be best if she joined us. Dawn?" Jason gestured to the stairs. "Why don't you take the lead?"

"Yes, absolutely. I want to hear every word you have to say to Dalton, so I can repeat it to his lawyer." Dawn looked back at Suzie and Mary. "You're not going to get away with this." She turned back and headed down the stairs.

"Do you really think Dalton is the one who took the gold?" Mary looked over at Suzie.

"You're the one that found it in his closet." Suzie met her eyes. "What do you think?"

"I don't know." Mary frowned. "To be honest, I'm not convinced. He looked shocked by the idea of there even being any missing gold."

"Dawn wasn't." Suzie clasped her hands behind her back. "What if she was looking for the gold herself? She came back here without the others."

"She'd have access to Dalton's room, that's for

sure. She barely ever leaves his side." Mary led Suzie down the stairs.

"But if she knew about that gold, I bet that Jason will get it out of her."

"The police need more than that." Mary sighed. "Even if they are able to figure out who took the gold, that still won't tell us who killed Jimmy."

"You're right. Charlie is still in custody, and he might confess. But honestly, I'm not certain that he is the one who killed Jimmy." Suzie pursed her lips, then rubbed the heel of her palm across her forehead. "All of this is completely out of control now. Soon, Wes and Paul will be back."

"Not soon, now." Mary looked towards the door as it swung open.

"That was probably the best ice cream I've ever tasted." Tiffany grinned as she walked through the door. "Sam, you still have some on your chin." She laughed as she swiped at his chin.

"Stop." Sam pushed her hand away, then wiped the ice cream off himself. "It was very good. Where's Dalton?" He looked straight at Mary. "He said that he was coming back here to get Dawn. Where are they?"

"Listen everyone, there have been some

developments." Suzie glanced at Paul, then looked back at Sam. "Dalton and Dawn are down at the police station for questioning. I'm sure whatever is going on, it will all be straightened out in no time."

"I'm going down there." Sam turned and stalked out of the house.

"Suzie, what happened?" Paul took a step closer to her.

"I'll tell you all about it." Suzie took a deep breath. "Tiffany, are you okay?"

"I'll be fine, once I'm in my room." Tiffany shook her head. "I've had enough of all of this chaos."

"Mary. Aren't we overdue for our walk?" Wes offered her his hand. "Why don't we get some fresh air?"

"That might be a good idea." Mary nodded as she looked over at Suzie. "We won't be long."

"Take your time, Mary. We may have to pick this up in the morning. I want to go down to the station and find out what is happening there." Suzie slipped her arm through Paul's. "I'll tell you everything on the way."

"Great, because it looks like there is a lot I need to catch up on." Paul nodded.

Wes led Mary out onto the porch, and then

down, across the sand, to the water's edge. He ran his hand along her shoulders as she looked out over the water.

"Take a few deep breaths. All of this is too much pressure on you."

"Oh, I can handle pressure." Mary turned to face him. "Wes, you said you wanted me to let you help me more, right?"

"I'd like that very much, yes." Wes smiled.

"Great. Because I want your help." Mary searched his eyes. "I want to go back down into the mine. I think we missed something, and I think with your experience as a detective, you might be able to figure out what it is."

"Mary, it's already been searched thoroughly." Wes shook his head.

"Not by us, it hasn't." Mary offered him her hand. "Are you going to help me or not?"

"Yes, I'll help you." Wes took her hand as his jaw rippled with tension. "But don't you want to go tomorrow when it's light?"

"I don't want to wait. You're working tomorrow. I want to go with you." Mary squeezed his hand.

"Okay. I have some flashlights in my car." Wes' expression grew serious. "But when I say it's time to go, it's time to go."

"I can agree to that." They headed towards Wes' car.

CHAPTER 18

When Suzie stepped through the door of the police station, she was greeted by the chaos that she expected. Sam's shouting echoed through the police station, while Dawn egged him on from right beside him. Several officers had clustered around the reception area in an attempt to deal with the disruption.

"I can see that things are definitely out of hand." Paul straightened his shoulders as he walked towards the group.

"No. We'll just add fuel to the fire." Suzie grabbed his hand and led him down the hall towards Jason's office. She almost walked straight into him when he stepped out of one of the interrogation rooms.

Suzie looked through the open door and noticed Charlie sitting in the middle of the room, handcuffed to a table.

"Suzie, what are you doing here?" Jason closed the door.

"I wanted to see what was happening with everything." Suzie nodded. "Did you get any information from Charlie?"

"No, he is denying knowing anything about the gold," Jason explained. "I have to let him go. I don't have enough to arrest him, and I can't hold him for much longer."

"There is so much evidence stacked up against him. How can you just let him walk out of here?" Suzie shook her head. "If you let him go, then you might never find out what really happened to Jimmy."

"Suzie, there's nothing I can do about it. The law is the law. I don't have enough to keep him, especially since the gold was found in Dalton's room. If you hadn't found it, I could try to keep him longer, but since you did, I have no proof that he was involved at all. There isn't any physical evidence tying him to the crime. If there was, the results would be quite different. As it is now, all we know for sure, is that the gold was in the closet in

SAND, SEA AND A SKELETON

Dalton's room. I have to start working that angle. When I put some pressure on Dalton, I'm sure he'll cave about his involvement with Charlie."

"It'll be too late by then." Suzie sighed.

"I can keep him for a couple more hours. Hopefully, I'll turn up something. As you can hear, things are escalating." Jason looked towards the lobby of the police station, where Sam still demanded to see Dalton. "I'll catch up with you later."

"This way, Paul." Suzie steered him out through a side door.

As they walked towards the car, Suzie tried to get hold of Mary to give her an update, but it went straight to voicemail. She left a message that they were on their way back and would update Mary then.

As Suzie drove back to Dune House she could barely hold in her frustration. "Whoever killed Jimmy is going to get away with it." She sighed.

"Suzie, take a breath." Paul looked over at her. "You don't know that. Jason will figure this out."

Suzie pulled into the parking lot of Dune House and parked near the side entrance. As she stepped out of the car, she felt uneasy. Paul opened the gate of the fenced-in area and Pilot ran up to say hello to them. Suzie bent down to pat him. If Pilot was still in the yard, then Suzie knew that Mary hadn't been back to Dune House.

"Something is not right, Paul." Suzie took his hand and led him up the porch and into the house. "Mary?"

The house remained quiet. She pulled out her phone and dialed Mary's number. When the call went to voicemail, again, she turned to face Paul.

"She's not answering. They should be back by now." Suzie narrowed her eyes as she paced the length of the dining room. "I don't see them anywhere." She peered down the beach, then she walked over to the window that overlooked the parking lot.

"Try to relax, Suzie. I'm sure they're both just fine. They're probably off doing something terribly romantic." Paul ran his hand along the length of her shoulders.

"No, you're wrong." Suzie spun around to face him. "Mary knows how tense everything is around here. She would never be out of contact with me for this long."

"Do you really think they're in trouble?" Paul's eyes locked to hers.

"Yes, I think they might be." Suzie sighed, then

pulled her phone out of her pocket again. "She hasn't called or texted me back. Neither has Wes. It's just not like them."

"If you're really concerned, then I think it's time we called Jason." Paul tipped his head towards her phone. "Do you want me to do it, or will you?"

"I'm not sure how much help Jason is going to be, he has his hands full, but I'll give it a try." Suzie dialed Jason's number. As she expected, it went to voicemail. She left a quick message about her concern. A few minutes later he called back.

"I put a trace on Mary's cell phone. I can't believe this, but the last place it pinged was near the mine. I've already sent some cars out there."

"Why would she go back there?" Suzie jumped as the windows rattled and the floor shook beneath her feet. "Paul!" She grabbed for his arm as he lunged towards her.

"It's okay," Paul murmured as he looked out through the window. "It looks like there was some kind of explosion." He pointed out the smoke that curled up into the sky over the woods.

"Oh no!" Suzie gasped. "That's the direction of the mine. We have to go, right now!" She ended the call and slid the phone into her pocket as she ran straight for the door. Paul rushed after her. All along the street, doors opened and people stuck their heads out, curious about the shaking, and the smoke in the sky. "It was the mine, I just know it was." Suzie's heart felt as if it was going to break free from her chest it was beating so hard. She held back tears as she drove to the main entrance of the mine.

"That doesn't mean that Mary and Wes were inside." Paul gritted his teeth as she took a sharp turn. "Suzie, we are not going to be able to help them if we run off the road before we can get to them."

"I'm sorry, you're right." Suzie slowed down as they arrived at the mine. She heard sirens in the distance. "The police officers that Jason sent out are coming." She stepped out of the car. Her nostrils burned in reaction to the smoke in the air. She was about to lunge for the entrance of the mine when she saw movement out of the corner of her eye. "Stop!" She shouted as she chased after the figure.

Paul passed by her and launched himself on top of the man. He pinned him down to the ground just as the police cars pulled up.

"Bob?" Paul gasped out, as he peered down at the man. "What are you doing here?"

"Look at his hands, Paul." Suzie crouched down. "They're smudged with dirt and gunpowder. Did you do this, Bob? Did you set off explosives in the mine?"

"Let him up!" Jason's commanding voice bellowed from a few feet behind them. He pointed a flashlight and his gun at Bob.

Paul eased off him and edged away from Jason and Bob, as Jason zeroed in on him.

"I didn't know there was anyone in there!" Bob gasped as he stumbled back from Jason's flashlight and drawn weapon. "I swear, I didn't! It was supposed to be empty!"

"What did you do, Bob?" Suzie rushed past Jason, towards the entrance of the mine.

"I was planting the explosives, and I heard them talking. I wanted to save them, but it was too late." Bob sank down to his knees. "The explosives had already been set and they went off before I could do anything. I just wanted all of this to be over." He clenched his hands into fists at his sides. "I made a terrible mistake. I never should have told Charlie about the gold. I never should have let any of this happen."

"Put your hands on top of your head." Jason continued to aim the gun and the flashlight beam in Bob's direction.

Suzie's heart pounded as she realized what Bob

meant. Mary and Wes were inside the mine, and the explosives had gone off. At the very least they were trapped, at the worst, they might already be gone. Suzie tore at the entrance of the mine.

"Don't." Paul pulled her back from it. "You can't get in through there, Suzie."

"Suzie, it's not safe. I'll have search and rescue here in no time." Jason clasped handcuffs over Bob's wrists. "Promise me you won't go in there." He looked into her eyes.

"Just get them here!" Suzie took off at a sprint around the side of the mine. She knew where the other entrance was. Maybe it wouldn't be blocked.

"Suzie wait!" Paul chased after her and caught up with her at the door. "He's right, we have no idea what we're getting into once we step into the mine."

"So what?" Suzie gasped out. "Mary and Wes are trapped in there! Do you really expect me to just leave them in there?"

"So, we need to be careful, and smart about this." Paul gazed into her eyes. "We'll go in together, with our flashlights on, and these." He grabbed two of the filthy helmets that had been left behind by the workers and handed one to Suzie. "Put it on."

Suzie didn't hesitate. She placed it on top of her

head, then pulled aside the brush. Paul caught her by the shoulder.

"Me first." Paul narrowed his eyes, prepared to argue.

Suzie nodded as her chest tightened. All she cared about was getting to Mary.

CHAPTER 19

"'m sorry, Mary, I can't move any more of the rocks." Wes' hands fell to his sides. "The explosion has blocked the exit."

"Wes, I'm sorry that I brought us down here." Mary's heart raced as she clung to his hand. The last flicker of light faded from her flashlight. "I never should have. I just wanted to do something to help."

"It's not your fault, Mary." Wes wrapped his arms around her and held her close. "You didn't do anything wrong. Don't give up hope. We're going to find our way out of here."

"How?" Mary sighed as she sank down onto the ground. Her heart pounded. "There isn't another way out. Both ends of the corridor are blocked off.

213

We came all the way down here, and all I found were these." She held out some blue marbles in her hand. "These aren't going to prove anything." Was she really going to die in a mine?

"Let's not worry about that now." Wes crouched down in front of her. "What we need to focus on is getting out of here."

"But how?" Mary's lip trembled.

"I'm not sure." Wes hugged her. "But we have to try."

"You're right." Mary pulled out her phone again. Her heart raced. The thought of not being able to escape the small, dark space was too terrible to even consider. "I still don't have any service. I should have told Suzie where we were going. Then at least she would be looking for us. I doubt they will even search the mine to see if anyone was inside."

"All that matters is that we know we're going to get out of here." Wes grabbed her hands and looked into her eyes. "Sweetheart, our story doesn't end like this. I don't know how it ends, and I don't know how we're getting out of here, but I know that we will."

"Wes." Mary sighed as she tightened her grasp on his hands. "I hope you're right."

"I know I am." Wes drew her hands to his lips

and kissed the back of each one. "They might not search for us, Mary, but they are going to come to find out what happened here. Do you hear those sirens?"

"They're so far away." Mary frowned.

"But they won't be for long. There will be a lot of people around the mine for at least a little while. They are going to investigate the explosion. So, what we have to do is make sure they know we're here." Wes stood up and walked over to the pile of rocks that blocked the door. Then he began to shout.

"Help! We're in here! Help!"

Mary pushed herself to her feet. She doubted that anyone would be able to hear them from outside the mine. But she had to try. As her voice joined Wes', she felt a faint glimmer of hope. Maybe he was right. Maybe there was a way out after all. She shouted until her voice was hoarse. Then she stopped. Wes banged his flashlight against the rocks as he took heavy breaths, worn out from shouting.

"No one's coming," Mary murmured. In the quiet that followed, she heard a distant sound. At first, she thought it had to be her imagination. Then she heard it again.

"Wes, shh!" Mary caught his hand to stop him from banging the flashlight. "Listen."

"Mary?" Suzie's voice drifted past the pile of rubble. "Mary, are you in there?"

"Wes!" Mary squeezed his hand. "Wes, Suzie is here!" She pressed her face close to the small opening between the rocks and called out as loud as she could. "Suzie! We're behind these rocks!"

"Mary, we're going to get you out. Just try to stay calm. It's going to take some time." Suzie paused, then she shouted louder. "Are you okay? Are you hurt? Is Wes okay?"

"We're okay." Wes called back. "We're both okay." He wrapped his arms around Mary's trembling body.

"We'll get you out of there soon, just sit tight." Paul's voice forced its way past the rocks.

It took quite some time, but the rocks were eventually moved out of the way. A rescue team guided Mary and Wes back out of the mine.

"Mary!" Suzie threw her arms around her the moment that she saw her. "I wanted to stay down there, but they wouldn't let me."

"It's okay." Mary hugged her tight as her voice quivered. "Thanks to you, we're safe. I didn't think anyone would come looking for us. It was so foolish of me to have gone down there. I just thought maybe we could find one bit of evidence that could crack the case. Instead, all I found are these." She opened her hand to show Suzie the marbles. "They don't mean anything."

"They look like something a child would play with." Suzie studied the marbles.

"I know." Mary nodded, then tucked them into her pocket. "Do you have any idea what happened? We were down in the mine and all of a sudden we heard explosions."

"Yes, I think I have a good idea of what happened now." Suzie looked into Mary's tear-filled eyes. "Do you think you can stand a trip down to the police station?" Jason had returned to the police station earlier, once he knew that Mary and Wes would be safe.

"Yes, I can. Why? I know that look in your eyes, Suzie. You've figured this out, haven't you?" Mary pulled away from their hug long enough to look into her friend's eyes.

"Maybe." Suzie frowned. "But only because of what you found."

"Back to the police station?" Paul shook his

head. "Why not? Let's just add to the chaos that's already happening there."

"I'm coming, too." Wes wrapped his arm around Mary's waist. "If that's okay with you?"

"Of course, it is." Mary smiled, then kissed his cheek.

When they reached the police station, Suzie found Jason.

"I need to talk to you, Jason." Suzie held his gaze. "I think I've finally figured this all out. Can you get everyone together?"

"If you explain exactly what is going on first." Jason looked at her. Suzie filled Jason, Mary, Wes and Paul in on her suspicions. "Okay." Jason nodded when she had finished. "That adds up. Give me a few minutes."

While Jason worked on gathering up everyone that he wanted at the meeting, Suzie and Mary discussed what they believed had happened. Jason returned to the lobby, then guided them to a large conference room. Inside were several police officers, along with Charlie, Sam, Dalton, Tiffany, Dawn, and Bob.

"All right, everybody, I think it's time to tell the truth." Jason looked straight at Charlie. "You'd better start talking, or you're going to be facing murder charges. Do you really want to spend the rest of your life in jail, Charlie?"

"I didn't do anything." Charlie scowled.

"Who told you about the gold, Charlie?" Jason narrowed his eyes. "This is your last chance. If you tell me everything, I can try and get you a reduced sentence. You should tell me exactly what happened. You don't want to go down for murder if you weren't involved. Do you?"

"Come on, Charlie." Dawn looked at him. "If you have something to hide, you should reveal it now. They will find out what happened eventually."

Charlie looked at the handcuffs on his wrists and sighed.

"I had nothing to do with Jimmy being killed. I never knew he was in there. Bob contacted me. He stayed friends with my son from when we were here, and they played a couple of games of basketball together." Charlie looked towards Bob then back to Jason. Bob sat with his head bowed in the corner. Suzie guessed he was still in shock from setting off the explosives that he thought might have killed Wes and Mary. "Bob told me that he knew where there was some gold stashed in the mine. He didn't know exactly where it was, but he had an idea. So, when Bob explained to me the area where the gold was, I knew exactly which corridor it would be down. I knew the corridor from when I went to talk to Jimmy. He took me down that corridor and said we wouldn't be disturbed there. Bob couldn't find the corridor. He said if I went in to get the gold, he would split it with me." He chuckled, then shook his head. "So, that's what I did. I decided to bring the walking group with me in case it was a trap, I would have witnesses to help defend me. I was going to check it out first, but Sam got nosy real fast. He must have sensed that I was looking for something. He made sure he was the first one into that corridor, and he looked inside the bag before anyone else came in. When I broke off from the group to go back to get the bag, he followed me. He said if I didn't split it with him, he would turn me in." He lifted his shoulders in a mild shrug. "I don't know how the gold got into Dalton's room."

"I put it there." Sam frowned as he looked over at his friend. "I'm sorry, Dalton. I didn't think anyone would suspect you, and I knew even if you came across it, you wouldn't try to steal it. It seemed like the safest place to store it."

"Are you kidding me?" Dalton glared at him. "Sam, I was about to go to prison. How could you do this to me, after everything that I've done for you?"

"That's why I'm telling the truth, now." Sam took a deep breath. "I'm sorry, Dalton. I know that you've always wanted me to be a better man than I am, but this is just all I am. I see an opportunity, and I take it. It was gold!"

"Sam." Dalton sighed.

"Did you delete the photos of the skeleton and the bag from my phone?" Tiffany asked Sam.

"I'm sorry." Sam cringed. "I had to get rid of the evidence of the bag. I thought, I hoped, that no one had noticed the bag, and if there were no pictures, then there was no chance of anyone proving the bag was there."

"How could you do all this, Sam?" Dalton shook his head. then he looked over at Jason. "I had nothing to do with any of this. Are you going to let me go?"

"Once everything is straightened out, if you had no part in this, then I will, of course." Jason looked over at Dawn. "How about you? Did you know anything about this?"

"Well, I—" Dawn cleared her throat.

"Dawn?" Dalton locked his eyes to hers. "Tell him you didn't know anything."

"I didn't exactly. It's just, I overheard Sam and Charlie talking, and I saw Sam sneak into Dalton's room. I kind of suspected that the gold might be in there. When everyone went out, I stayed behind to see if I could find it." Dawn blushed as she looked down at her feet. "I just wanted to protect you, Dalton."

"If that was true, you would have told me about it." Dalton narrowed his eyes.

"I didn't know what to do. I didn't want to get Sam in trouble, I mean, he's your friend." Dawn clasped her hands together. "I'm sorry, Dalton."

"This is ridiculous." Dalton looked over at Mary. "So, who was it that trapped you in the mine? I know that Sam wouldn't have done it. He may be opportunistic, but he's not a killer."

"It was Bob." Mary took a deep breath. "But he did it to protect his father." She met Jason's eyes. "I have reason to believe that Donald killed Jimmy. Donald had been stashing the extra gold in the mine, and Jimmy found it. That's why the gold was in a bag from the gym that Donald owned. Jimmy was going to tell Terrance that Donald was ripping him off by stealing from the mine. So before he could, Donald wanted to get rid of Jimmy. He shot Jimmy, and Jimmy fled into the mine with the gold. He ended up in a corridor that Donald didn't know about. Only the workers did. It wasn't on the layout drawings for the mine, but the workers had come across it when they worked there. That's where he died, and Donald couldn't find him or the gold. He thought he must have escaped with it. He couldn't ask the workers to look for it, because then they would suspect him and might even find Jimmy's dead body."

"But with no witnesses, there's no way to prove that." Wes spoke up as he draped an arm around Mary's shoulders.

"There was a witness." Suzie pulled out her phone. She flipped to the picture of the little boy holding a gold nugget. "Bob was in that mine when his father shot Jimmy. That's how he knew the gold was there. He used to explore the mine. He knew that Jimmy and the gold were hidden down there. He hoped that Charlie would know the secret passageway from when he met Jimmy there. He had seen Jimmy take Charlie towards the area where Jimmy eventually went missing. Bob gave the information about where the gold might be to Charlie because all of his businesses were failing. He couldn't stand the idea of the mine being sold with the gold still in it. Isn't that right, Bob?" She watched as he started to squirm in his handcuffs.

"This is all nonsense!" Bob growled. "That gold was in our mine, my father still owns it, which means it belongs to us!"

"Not so fast." Jason grabbed him by the arm. "You only have one chance to get out of this without spending the rest of your life in jail, Bob. You're going to tell me everything you know about the day that Jimmy was shot, who pulled the trigger, and why. Kirk." Jason tipped his head towards the other detective in the room. "You need to go pick up Donald right away."

"Yes, fine." Bob sighed. "I was there. I was playing with my marbles, and I heard the shots. Then I saw Jimmy run past me. Then I saw my father run after him. I was scared, so I hid. My father looked for hours, but he couldn't find Jimmy. I've never told my father I was there that day. I didn't know where Jimmy was, I knew there were some secret passages in the mines, that only the workers knew about." He lowered his eyes.

"So, you decided to blow up the mine to destroy any evidence that might point to your father. But you wanted the gold first." Jason nodded as he studied the man. "You used Charlie to get it out of the mine, because he knew where to go to find Jimmy. He knew the secret passageway, and you hoped he would be able to find it."

"Yes." Bob hung his head. "It was our gold. We needed it. And, I thought if Charlie found Jimmy's skeleton, then he would be blamed for killing him. Then I wouldn't have to split the gold, and my father wouldn't be suspected of Jimmy's murder."

"You're a slippery fellow, aren't you?" Charlie glared at him.

"I think it's time we go home, Suzie and Mary." Paul looked at them, as Jason led Bob out of the conference room. An officer followed him with Sam, and Dalton in tow. Another officer brought Charlie, Dawn and Tiffany. "I think Jason is going to have a lot of paperwork to do."

"Home sounds good." Suzie nodded.

"Yes, it does." Mary and Wes followed after them.

"Suzie, are you okay?" Paul gazed at her. "It's been a wild night."

"I'm fine." Suzie looked over at Mary and Wes. "Now that they're safe, I am fine."

"Do you think they'll release him?" Mary watched as Dalton was led to a different room from the others.

"I'm sure Jason will." Suzie nodded. "He's not in the business of arresting innocent people. My guess is Charlie won't be behind bars long, and neither will Sam or Dawn. But I imagine that Donald and maybe even Bob, will be. At least, we finally know the truth about what happened to Jimmy."

"Yes, we do." Mary took Suzie's hand. "He has his justice, even if it was a long time coming."

"Mary, I have a very important question to ask you." Wes stepped in front of her and gazed into her eyes.

"You do?" Mary raised an eyebrow.

"All of that adrenaline in the mine." Wes shook his head. "I'm starving. Is there any of that soup left?"

Everyone laughed as Mary rolled her eyes.

"Yes, of course. I'll warm some up as soon as we get back." Mary headed for the parking lot with Wes' arm around her waist.

Suzie smiled as she nestled close to Paul.

"You know, I do love it when you're on dry land." She tipped her head to the side as she looked up at him.

"So do I." Paul leaned down to give her a light kiss. "Something tells me, I need to keep a closer eye on you."

"You think?" Suzie grinned. "Maybe I'll just find another abandoned mine to explore."

"Or, we could just have some soup." Paul took her hand and led her towards the car.

The End

ALSO BY CINDY BELL

DUNE HOUSE COZY MYSTERIES

NUTS ABOUT NUTS COZY MYSTERIES

A Tough Case to Crack

A Seed of Doubt

Roasted Peanuts and Peril

Chestnuts, Camping and Culprits

WAGGING TAIL COZY MYSTERIES

Murder at Pawprint Creek (prequel)

Murder at Pooch Park

Murder at the Pet Boutique

A Merry Murder at St. Bernard Cabins

Murder at the Dog Training Academy

Murder at Corgi Country Club

CHOCOLATE CENTERED COZY MYSTERIES

The Sweet Smell of Murder

A Deadly Delicious Delivery

A Bitter Sweet Murder

A Treacherous Tasty Trail

Pastry and Peril

Trouble and Treats

Fudge Films and Felonies

Custom-Made Murder

Skydiving, Soufflés and Sabotage

Christmas Chocolates and Crimes

Hot Chocolate and Homicide

Chocolate Caramels and Conmen

Picnics, Pies and Lies

Devils Food Cake and Drama

Cinnamon and a Corspe

Cherries, Berries and a Body

DONUT TRUCK COZY MYSTERIES

Deadly Deals and Donuts

Fatal Festive Donuts

Bunny Donuts and a Body

Strawberry Donuts and Scandal

Frosted Donuts and Fatal Falls

SAGE GARDENS COZY MYSTERIES

Birthdays Can Be Deadly

Money Can Be Deadly

Trust Can Be Deadly

Ties Can Be Deadly

Rocks Can Be Deadly

Jewelry Can Be Deadly

Numbers Can Be Deadly

Memories Can Be Deadly

Paintings Can Be Deadly

Snow Can Be Deadly

Tea Can Be Deadly

Greed Can Be Deadly

Clutter Can Be Deadly

BEKKI THE BEAUTICIAN COZY MYSTERIES

Hairspray and Homicide

A Dyed Blonde and a Dead Body

Mascara and Murder

Pageant and Poison

Conditioner and a Corpse

Mistletoe, Makeup and Murder

Hairpin, Hair Dryer and Homicide

Blush, a Bride and a Body

Shampoo and a Stiff

Digging for Dirt

WENDY THE WEDDING PLANNER COZY
MYSTERIES

Matrimony, Money and Murder

Chefs, Ceremonies and Crimes

Knives and Nuptials

Mice, Marriage and Murder

ABOUT THE AUTHOR

Cindy Bell is a USA Today and Wall Street Journal Bestselling Author. She is the author of the cozy mystery series Wagging Tail, Donut Truck, Dune House, Sage Gardens, Chocolate Centered, Macaron Patisserie, Nuts about Nuts, Bekki the Beautician, Heavenly Highland Inn and Wendy the Wedding Planner.

Cindy has always loved reading, but it is only recently that she has discovered her passion for writing romantic cozy mysteries. She loves walking along the beach thinking of the next adventure her characters can embark on.

You can sign up for her newsletter so you are notified of her latest releases at http://www.cindybellbooks.com.

Made in the USA
Las Vegas, NV
20 May 2023